Pray Elk River leaders from left to right.
Percy Kallevig, Gene Rick, Bob Pullar, Paul Salfrank,
Greg Pagh, Jay Bunker, Dave Johnson, Chuck Ripka, Ken Beaudry.

Picture by Tanner Ripka.
Taken Tuesday, February 17, 2004,
at the noon time prayer meeting.

PRAISE FOR
THE ELK RIVER STORY

Let's all keep our eyes on Elk River, Minnesota. Rick Heeren's *The Elk River Story* is an exciting, revealing, faith-building account of how church and workplace leaders together can tap into God's power for social transformation.

C. Peter Wagner, Chancellor, Colorado Springs, Colorado
Wagner Leadership Institute

• •

The Elk River Story is a contemporary narrative that had to be written and MUST be read! God wants to transform whole regions, nations, and even continents. But for this to happen, cities and towns have to be reached first. This is the great challenge and encouragement of *The Elk River Story*. Read, learn, and picture the transformation of your own hometown and nation.

Roger Mitchell
Passion, London, England; Co-leader of Target Europe

• •

The spiritual transformation of a city or region in the United States is no longer just a theory. It is happening in Elk River, Minnesota. Reading these reports will encourage and strengthen the effort of the rapidly growing numbers of men and women across America, and around the world, who are believing spiritual transformation will occur in their communities. After reading *The Elk River Story*, I'm more convinced than ever that when the spiritual leadership in a geographic region is represented by more than the pastors, the church will become the powerful presence Jesus said it should be. These testimonies are from pastors, prayer intercessors, business people, and even the city's mayor. This is a story of the Body of Christ working together to create a culture of transformation. It is the church being God's redemptive community and changing the spiritual climate of a city. This story gives us new hope for the transformation of our nation.

John Isaacs, San Jose, California
Senior Pastor, South Bay Covenant Church
President, Pray The Bay

It is possible to see the spiritual climate over a city be changed, even in the Western world! *The Elk River Story* is a series of faith inspiring testimonies from the people who have been and are in the midst of a process of transforming their city. They come from all walks of life, but are united in the desire to see Christ lifted up in all areas of the life of Elk River. This book will encourage other city reachers and even inspire others to embrace a new vision to touch their cities for Christ.

Dr. Reidar Paulsen
Senior Pastor Christ Church, Bergen, Norway
Co-leader of the Pastoral Network in Bergen, called Pray Bergen

• •

This book comes at the right time. We need to hear what God is doing - bringing unity to a city in order to bring salvation. This is a great book and I can identify with the process in this city. We are seeing some of the same results in Bergen, Norway. We had a vision to see our city changed and God gave us the strategy of prayer evangelism. *The Elk River Story* is encouraging because they are ahead of us in the process and are showing us that we are on the right track. I love to see the people of God moving forward to let whole cities and nations see the glory of God.

Noralv Askeland
Senior Pastor, Christian Fellowship, Bergen, Norway
Co-leader of the Pastoral Network in Bergen, called Pray Bergen

• •

This book edited by Rick Heeren is a must-read for all those who desire to see transformation happen in their cities and / or nations. If you have watched the *Transformations* videos, and you would like it to happen in your city and nation, this book has captured and outlined the step-by-step process of transformation using prayer evangelism as the strategy.

King Flores, Las Pinas City, Manila, Philippines
Pastor for Body Ministry, BF Homes Bible Church

In *The Elk River Story* we are given a practical demonstration of God the Father responding to the prayer of Jesus for the unity of his disciples, "that the world may know you have sent me" (John 17). Here is tremendous encouragement for those of us who have a burden for restoration of the Kingdom of God in our communities, but have yet to see the realisation of this in practice. It appears that no facet of city or social life remains untouched as we read account after account of transformation in place after place, beginning with the House of the Lord. Through this story our Father in Heaven once again reveals his compassion for every member of society, bar none. Truly inspiring!

Gordon Shewan, Aberdeen, Scotland
Senior Pastor, All Nations Christian Fellowship

• •

The call to reach the whole of our cities for Christ's Kingdom has grown stronger in the last decade. It is now at an all time high. Every city has its own DNA, but it is wonderful to have documented the story of Elk River. This justifies the pioneer call of those God raised up with the City Reaching message and articulated that. I believe many will be encouraged to press in for their city by reading the story of Elk River. It is also a tribute to the tenacity of Rick & Rachel Heeren who have believed the message for their area. I commend them and the story to you believing we will all be encouraged by the story they have edited and helped to put together.

David Brown, Sunderland, England
Pastor & City Reacher

• •

This is an amazing collection of stories of humble servants who have said *No* to ego and *Yes* to the call of Christ—crucified and risen. I long for this type of unity to come to the community I'm serving. *The Elk River Story* is nothing other than a fresh release of the Holy Spirit enabling surrendered leaders from many walks of life the privilege of knowing and being known, loving and being loved, serving and being served, celebrating and being celebrated. I believe Christ is smiling on Elk River.

Blair Anderson, Ramsey, Minnesota
Senior Pastor, Lord of Life Church

If your heart's desire is to see the church unified for kingdom advancement spurred by pastors, business people, intercessors, city officials and educators who love and trust one another, I commend to you the principles you will find in *The Elk River Story*. I know you will find encouragement and the call of God to see your city reached for Christ.

Randy Discher, Andover, Minnesota
Senior Pastor, Constance Evangelical Free Church

• •

The Elk River Story is more than a story. It is a move of God. As a pastor in the suburbs south of Elk River, God used this story as a catalyst to move the churches in our area. Two pastors, a businessman / prayer intercessor and a governmental leader in the Spring of 2001 shared how God was at work in Elk River. Their simple testimonies helped to develop a similar story that the Spirit is writing in the far western suburbs of Minneapolis. I thank God for Rick Heeren and his wife, Rachel, who have given their lives to assist the many stories the Spirit is creating throughout the Twin Cities.

Dr. Kevin D. Meyer, Medina, Minnesota
Senior Associate Pastor, Woodridge Church

• •

For all, like myself, who want to do God's will and be a part of what God is doing today and see the power of God manifested in their life, church and community, this collection of current testimonies and vision given in *The Elk River Story* will fan the flame and stir up the zeal needed to finish the race set before you. Rick Heeren is an emerging author who has a gift to encourage the church to accomplish the mission of evangelism given to it. This book is a testimony that the prayer of Jesus in John 17 for Christ centered unity can happen city wide. A must-read in staying abreast with the current revival.

Steve Thompson, Bemidji, Minnesota
Senior Pastor, Mount Zion Church

It is my joy and privilege to encourage everyone to experience the amazing story of what God is doing through prayer evangelism in the city of Elk River, Minnesota. *The Elk River Story* is a compilation of events and experiences written by various pastors and leaders of the community who share the profound workings of God as they are happening in their city. It is truly a work of His grace and something to be desired by every pastor and leader for their communities. Rick and Rachel Heeren have carefully documented every step of this renewal which will capture your imagination and faith and bring the reader to a new hunger and hope for revival in their own cities. After pastoring for 36 years in the Shell Lake area, I am excited to see the beginnings of similar manifestations here of the kind of revival which is now happening in Elk River. This book will bring new hope to your vision.

Virgil Amundson, Shell Lake, Wisconsin
Senior Pastor, Shell Lake Full Gospel Church

• •

God has been waiting for a long time for us to retake the cities of the world for Christ Jesus! This can only be done as we follow the pattern of blessing that Jesus commands! I was challenged and stretched by this book because I have known the power of both a blessing and of a curse. I choose in Jesus to walk the way of the blessing and purpose to recommend this biblical model to you who really want Jesus to be Lord of your city!

John Mehrens, Granby, Missouri
Senior Pastor, Granby Christian Church

• •

The true grit of *The Elk River Story* is the play-by-play reality of how the Kingdom of God is advanced in a city when obedient men and women take God out of the "church box." When determined people buy into God's idea of evangelism, every facet of society is impacted. A must-read for culture changers.

Dr. Phil Nordin, Calgary, Alberta, Canada
International Association of Ministries

The Elk River Story is a practical, deeply inspiring model of what God will set in motion when there is genuine love, unity, prayer and bold practical ministry action steps taken by dedicated community leaders. The Gospel of Jesus Christ is being powerfully communicated and demonstrated daily though local marketplace networks and far beyond. Read these pages carefully and hear what the Lord would have you do as an agent of transformation in your city!

Jarry Cole, Minneapolis, Minnesota
Senior Pastor, RiverCity Outreach

• • • • • • • • • • • • • • • • • • • •

The Elk River Story is a great book! I am particularly drawn to the idea that the church is supposed to be a resource to our public officials. The idea that there should be separation between church and state is a lie from the devil. Ask the Police Chief in Elk River how he caught the drug dealers in his city—he caught them when the church prayed. Ask the Superintendent of Schools how he got a referendum passed to refurbish the schools—the referendum passed when the church prayed. Yes, we have to stop listening to the lie. Like the Riverview Bank in Otsego, our institutions need to be centered on the phrase—In God We Trust!

Larry Ihle, Farmington, Minnesota
Business Owner and CEO, Dexterity Dental Arts

THE ELK RIVER STORY

Transforming the spiritual climate of a city

CONTRIBUTING WRITERS

Carrie Beaudry
Ken Beaudry
Jay Bunker
Debbie DeLong
K. C. Foster
Rick Heeren
Percy Kallevig
Stephanie Klinzing
Pam Kringlund
Tom Ness
Greg Pagh
Bob Pullar
Chuck Ripka
Paul Salfrank
Dave Thompson

COMPILED & EDITED BY RICK HEEREN

First printing: February 2004.
Printed in the United States of America.

Published by Transformational Publications
A division of Harvest Evangelism, Inc.
P.O. Box 20310, San Jose, CA 95160-0310
Tel. 408-927-9052
www.harvestevan.org

ISBN 0-9752823-1-X

Dedication

Dedicated to my dear friend and mentor Ed Silvoso.

He told me that I had an anointing to pray for businesses.
I believed him, I tried it, and miracles happened.

He told me that whole cities could be transformed
through prayer evangelism.
He told me that the City of Elk River would be a prototype.
I believed him and urged others to believe it and to try it.
Together we have seen the spiritual climate
in Elk River transformed.

What a blessing it is to have someone in your life
who encourages you to stretch way outside yourself
and to believe that nothing is impossible for God.
He has truly raised the bar of expectations
that I have for my life.

ACKNOWLEDGMENTS

I want to acknowledge the significant contributions that were made to *The Elk River Story* by two of my former colleagues, Eric Straub and David Sluka. They both spent countless hours and days in Elk River and Otsego, working behind the scenes to bring encouragement and support to the leaders of Pray Elk River.

I also want to acknowledge the help that Dave Thompson, Senior Vice President of Harvest Evangelism in our headquarters in San Jose, California, has provided in the editing of this manuscript. His many years of experience, his knowledge of the subject of prayer evangelism, and his great wisdom have added immeasurably to the quality of this effort.

My thanks to David Sluka for preparing the interior of this book and for reviewing the final product from the perspective of his considerable experience in Elk River. He and Cindy Oliveira also gave me great assistance in making many valuable last minute changes.

I also want to express my gratitude to John Hanka for his excellent work in designing the cover for the book.

Rick Heeren

CONTENTS

Foreword

Those who have watched George Otis, Jr.'s *Transformations* video are usually left with a longing to see in their cities what this documentary portrays. The most dramatic example of radical transformation in this video is Almolonga, a Guatemalan community where even the weather and the soil have been radically improved. But the transformation of Almolonga did not happen in just one day, or in a week or even in a year. The ocean at high tide we see portrayed in the video began with the silent initial tremor of a tsunami in the deepest part of the sea. Unfortunately, no one was there to document the initial tremors.

In *The Elk River Story*, Rick Heeren, along with leading pulpit and marketplace ministers of Elk River and the surrounding communities, documents the origins and tracks the emergence of a transformation movement that has the potential to emulate Almolonga's. Elk River, Minnesota, with a population of about 20,000, has been experiencing the power of God for a few years now. This began when pastors and community leaders first came together to pray, and it took off when they chose to pastor the entire city instead of just their congregations. Later on it moved into high gear when the marketplace began to experience transformation, first at City Hall and then in the schools, the law enforcement, and businesses in general. Since then it has gained what looks like unstoppable momentum with a Christian bank opening its doors in nearby Otsego, impacting the lives of people on a daily basis.

My team and I have had the privilege of seeing this from the enviable perspective of ground zero when the pastors first invited us to come alongside them to launch a city reaching thrust in 1995. From the very beginning we have been impressed by the transparency and humility of these godly men and women at the helm of what God is doing in Elk River and the surrounding communities. These leaders will be the first ones to caution us not to overstate what is happening—that what we see today is just a beginning. It is refreshing to see this godly attitude. However, for those of us who travel the world facilitating city reaching movements, Elk River is a most promising work in progress. It is like a healthy embryo—still inside the womb but growing by the day.

I am so excited that Rick Heeren and both the pulpit and marketplace ministers in Elk River and the surrounding communities have taken the time, and the risk, to share their perspective on what God is doing in these communities. If things continue to move forward, in the future many students of city transformation will be grateful to them for having documented the initial, humble and at times feeble tremor that eventually came to the surface as a majestic tsunami.

It is my prayer that everyone who reads this book will be touched by the genuineness and transparency of the contributors, and that the biblical principles behind the emerging transformation in Elk River will arrest them in order to instill hope and empower them to implement these truths in their own cities.

Read and rejoice. As you do, be aware that the only thing that can kill faith is the absence of works since faith without works is dead. Consequently, take what you learn from these pages and put it into practice—today!

Ed Silvoso
Author, *That None Should Perish*

CHAPTER 1
PREFACE
BY RICK HEEREN

Ed Silvoso called me in late 1999 and said that he felt that there were to be four cities in the USA where Harvest Evangelism was already working which would be so successful in their implementation of prayer evangelism that they would detonate other cities to follow their example. He said that one of those four cities would be Elk River, Minnesota. I contacted Pastor Paul Salfrank, who is the lead pastor of Pray Elk River, and asked if he and the other leaders would pray about the idea of becoming a detonator city. They agreed to pursue that goal.

Early in 2000, the Midwest Regional team of Harvest Evangelism began working with them to accelerate the implementation of prayer evangelism in their city. The results were so positive that by early 2001 we were repeatedly asked to tell the Elk River story to other groups of pastors and leaders. After one of those presentations I felt that the Lord was urging me to work with these leaders to write The Elk River Story.

My city, God's city

Ed Silvoso wrote a booklet by this name in 2000. The subtitle of that booklet is *How to Change the Spiritual Climate Over Your City*. The first Scripture that Ed quotes is 2 Corinthians 4:4. I have added verse 3 for additional clarity,

But even if our gospel is veiled, it is veiled to those who

> are perishing, whose minds the god of this age has blinded, who do not believe, lest the light of the gospel of the glory of Christ, who is the image of God, should shine on them.

Scripture shows us that the reason that the spiritual climate is not conducive to evangelism is that the god of this age, or satan, has blinded the minds of unbelievers.

The second verse that Ed quotes is Acts 26:17-18 (NIV):

> I will rescue you from your own people and from the Gentiles. I am sending you to them to open their eyes and turn them from darkness to light, and from the power of satan to God, so that they may receive forgiveness of sins and a place among those who are sanctified by faith in me.

The essence of this Scripture is that the Lord sent *Paul,* and indeed He is sending *us* to open the eyes of those whom the god of this age blinded.

Ed says that prayer changes the spiritual climate and he offers 1 Timothy 2:1-2 as evidence:

> Therefore I exhort first of all that supplications, prayers, intercessions, *and* giving of thanks be made for all men, for kings and all who are in authority, that we may lead a quiet and peaceable life in all godliness and reverence.

Here is what Ed says about this Scripture:

> Paul tells us that if we pray for everybody, including those

> who are in authority, we will see a dramatic improvement in the spiritual atmosphere ... For godliness to increase in a city, ungodliness must decrease, and it cannot happen without radically improving the spiritual climate of the city.[1]

Ed further directs us to Luke 10:

> Jesus calls for us to do four things for the lost. It is very important for us to understand that the steps are interconnected and that to be effective they must be implemented in the order given:
>
> 1. Speak peace to the lost: Blessing opens the door to unbiased fellowship.
> 2. Fellowship with them: Fellowship establishes a level of trust, allowing our neighbors to share with us their felt needs.
> 3. Take care of their needs: Prayer addresses these felt needs.
> 4. Proclaim good news: When we intercede for our neighbors, God comes near them in a tangible way: "Say to them, 'The kingdom of God has come near to you'" (Luke 10:9).[2]

The objective of this Biblical approach is to see satan fall like lightening from the heavenlies (Luke 10:18) so that everyone in the city is forcing their way into the kingdom of God (Luke 16:16).

The second half of *My City, God's City* is the strategy for how to change the spiritual climate over a city. There are three components and these have been implemented in Elk River and the surrounding area.

1. Seven Steps to Cohesiveness
2. Seven Day Prayer Evangelism Outreach
3. Continuous City-wide Prayer Evangelism Thrust.[3]

Inclusiveness versus cohesiveness

Ed Silvoso comments on this topic as follows:

> Our experience shows that many, if not all, effective city reaching efforts began with and continue to be linked to a small but cohesive group of pastors and spiritual leaders who have covenanted together to model a process designed to bring the kingdom of God to the city.[4]

Seven steps to cohesiveness

Here are the seven steps:

1. Commit *yourself* to a personal lifestyle of prayer evangelism.
2. Engage *your family* in the same exercise with you.
3. Enlist and train *your leaders* to do the same.
4. Show your leaders how to engage *their families* in the process as you did with yours.
5. Recruit and equip *your workers* in the effort.
6. Mobilize your workers to enlist *their families*.
7. Bring the *participating congregations* together in a Celebration of Unity.[5]

These seven steps were accomplished in Elk River and the surrounding communities between 1999 and September 25, 2000 when they began the Seven Day Prayer Evangelism

Launch. I will cover this in much greater detail in Chapter 12, "A Week That Changed The City." For the purpose of this chapter, I simply want to tie this event back to the *My City, God's City* strategy.

The five components of the Seven Day Prayer Evangelism Launch include the following:

1. Celebration of Unity
2. Lighthouse of Prayer Radio Exercise
3. Intercession Emphasis
4. Door to door visitation
5. Prayer Fair[6]

Continuous city-wide prayer evangelism thrust

This component of the strategy involves the identification of seven groups of people within the participating congregations. These seven groups are as follows:

1. Pastors
2. Intercessors
3. Youth
4. Worshipers
5. Business leaders
6. Educational leaders
7. Government leaders[7]

My intention here is not to replicate the *My City, God's City* booklet. I simply want to acquaint the reader with these subjects. The important thing to note about the seven groups that must be engaged in a continuous city-wide prayer evangelism thrust is that *pastors aren't the only ones involved.* This seven component strategy is more like an orchestra than a solo performance.

The Elk River Story is a continuing saga, an unfinished book, an ongoing adventure. You will hear the heartbeat of several of the key players that are making Pray Elk River happen as they join me in sharing the ongoing adventure with you.

We begin with K.C. Foster, who was the very first contact that I had in Elk River.

Endnotes

1. Silvoso, Ed, *My City, God's City, How to Change the Spiritual Climate Over Your City,* Self published, San Jose, 2000, page 6.
2. Silvoso, ibid., page 7.
3. Silvoso, ibid., page 24.
4. Silvoso, ibid., page 25.
5. Silvoso, ibid., page 28.
6. Silvoso, ibid., page 30.
7. Silvoso, ibid., page 33.

CHAPTER 2

Conceived in the Marketplace

BY K.C. FOSTER

God has been working through many people in the Elk River area for quite some time. Various individuals and congregations have been praying for years that revival would happen in this area. Many individual congregations have had meetings and services focusing on prayer and renewal. There have been countless prayer and fellowship gatherings by small groups of people throughout our region. A few years ago a group of marketplace Christians put up a highway billboard leading into our city which said, "Jesus Christ is Lord over Elk River." The foundation for revival in the Elk River area has been built by many people over many years.

I am a marketplace Christian in the health and life insurance industry. In 1988, two marketplace Christians started to disciple me over the lunch hour one day each week. Fifteen years later we are still meeting, praying and sharing the Good News of Jesus Christ. In June of 1990, I accepted Jesus Christ to not only be my Savior, but also my Lord. I gave him control of my entire life and he directs my footsteps day by day.

One of my mentors decided to chair a committee for bringing the Lowell Lundstrom Crusade to Elk River. When the decision was made in July of 1994, my mentor felt that I should be the chairman of the Finance Committee. I resisted initially, but did agree to the position later on. This turned out to be one of the best God-led decisions that I have made in my life. Through this role I was able to get to know many of the pastors in the Elk River area. Familiarity with these pastors enabled the next move of God in my life.

In January of 1995, my life changed forever when I met Rick Heeren. We spent two and a half hours together over lunch as he related the concept of reaching whole cities for Christ through prayer evangelism. There are moments in your life when you know that the Holy Spirit is speaking directly to you. For me this was one of those moments. I knew this was from the Lord and I had to do something about it.

Rick told me about Ed Silvoso's book, *That None Should Perish* (Regal Books, 1994) and how the book laid out a plan for reaching entire cities for Christ. I bought two cases with the plan to give one copy to every pastor in Elk River and the surrounding area. In reading the book over the next few days, the Holy Spirit confirmed in me that taking one book to every pastor was exactly what God wanted. The Holy Spirit put a desire in me comparable to Psalm 133:1-3,

> Behold, how good and how pleasant *it is* For brethren to dwell together in unity!
> *It is* like the precious oil upon the head, Running down on the beard, The beard of Aaron, Running down on the edge of his garments.
> *It is* like the dew of Hermon, Descending upon the mountains of Zion; For there the LORD commanded the bless-

ing—Life forevermore.

Because of my contact with the pastors during the Lundstrom Crusade, it was natural for me to go and visit them. The first thing I did was to give a copy of the book to those I knew best. I urged them to read it and begin praying together. Those I didn't know were also given a book with the same recommendation of praying together. Every pastor in the Elk River area was given a book and a chance to respond.

Almost immediately one pastor felt this was of God and agreed to join the pastoral prayer group. Shortly after that another pastor agreed to pray with us. So Pastor Paul Salfrank, Pastor Bob Pullar, and I set aside one hour a month for prayer. Before long, another marketplace Christian joined us. Then one by one other pastors came to check out what was going on. They began clearing their calendars for the once a month prayer meeting. Unity was beginning to take root.

We decided to meet twice per month and changed the day to Tuesdays to allow more pastors to join. Soon, twice per month wasn't enough so weekly meetings became the norm. When that wasn't enough, day-long retreats started to happen. God was definitely building a solid foundation of prayer and unity. We came together in the name of the Lord Jesus Christ. We came to understand that there is only one Church in Elk River and Jesus Christ is the pastor of that Church. Jesus Christ is the Chief Shepherd, with many under-shepherds pastoring individual congregations.

Doctrinally we all didn't agree on everything, but we did agree on Jesus Christ being the one true Shepherd. With that as our foundation we started building. Our motto was: "Maintain unity in the essentials, tolerance in the nonessentials, love in both."

We started having celebrations of unity where the participating pastors would invite their congregations to an evening of prayer and praise for the sake of building unity. Invitations went out city-wide through our local newspaper and by word-of-mouth. People would come from almost all the congregations in the area and some came from outside the Elk River area. The Lord was spreading this news of unity to the other cities nearby and throughout the Twin Cities.

Not too long after that, the Lord showed us that an intercessory group needed to begin praying together. The invitation went out through the participating congregations that city-wide prayer would be on Monday evenings in the public library. Immediately many people responded and the intercessory prayer group started to function. These prayer warriors would pray for the pastors and in turn the pastors would pray for the intercessors. It was exciting to be a part of both. The pastors began to see themselves as gatekeepers and opened the doors for the Holy Spirit to come to the Elk River area in a powerful way. The intercessory group zeroed in on the Holy Spirit's desires and leading. Each week the intercessory group grew in numbers, and as more people joined, the Spirit of God started to reveal what needed to be done next.

This group of prayer warriors developed a strategy of prayer that specifically targeted certain areas. First on the list was to organize a number of three-person teams. Each team included a driver, a prayer captain, and a scribe. The scribe was there to record what the Holy Spirit revealed. The teams were first sent to all the entry points of the Elk River area. This included the following: all the roadways leading into the area, the railroad tracks, the three rivers running through the area, and the air which included airplanes, radio, and newspaper. It was amazing what God revealed through these drives to the entry points. All these intercessors were from many different congregations, but were united in purpose to bring the kingdom of Jesus Christ to our area.

The Holy Spirit revealed that we needed to research the history of the Elk River area. The way God would have it, we had a couple in our group who had done this same thing in another part of the country. We commissioned Walt and Barb Sukut to begin researching and writing the history for the area. More on that a bit later.

Meanwhile, the prayer continued as teams went out into the area on Monday nights praying for all of the following: all the congregations, all the government buildings and offices including county sheriff's department, city police and city fire, all the schools, public and private (preschools, elementary, junior high, and senior high schools), and finally all of the businesses. This was no small task and took quite a while, but these intercessors were committed and determined. In the Spirit realm, they accomplished great victories. None of them will take credit for any of it for they know that all the glory, all the honor, all the power, and all the praise goes to the Lord Jesus Christ.

While all this was going on, we were all being trained in the prayer evangelism process by the Harvest Evangelism team—by Ed Silvoso on the international/national level and by Rick Heeren on the local/regional level. We had many workshops on Lighthouses of Prayer, expanding the perimeter, unity celebrations, and much more. This was all outlined in the book, *That None Should Perish.* (Let me share a word of insight here. Every application from this book needs to follow the prompting and leading of the Holy Spirit. So it may look a little different from city to city, but the same basic principles will need to be in place.)

Walt and Barb Sukut finished the history of the Elk River area from 1700 to 1925 and presented it to the pastors and to the intercessory group. This is a crucial step for every area to do since it is vitally important to know things that happened in the past that need to be addressed through prayer. Through this process, the Lord taught us how to use identificational repentance to remove iniquities that happened earlier in history that were affecting our city in the present day. All I can say is, "WOW!"

We in the Elk River area want to thank the Harvest Evangelism team, Ed and Ruth Silvoso, Dave and Sue Thompson, Rick and Rachel Heeren, Eric and Caryl Straub*, David and Christina Sluka* , and many others. Without their guidance and leadership none of this would have happened. It is awesome to know that God will use each person who is willing to follow the leading of the Holy Spirit. All the glory, honor, and praise goes to Jesus. We are hearing from the Spirit, "You haven't seen nothing yet!" Get ready world, revival is coming.

* Former team members who remain friends of the vision and the ministry

CHAPTER 3
BIRTHED BY PASTORS

BY PASTOR PAUL SALFRANK

I am the pastor of a Christian and Missionary Alliance congregation within the church of Elk River and the surrounding area. Jesus said that His sheep listen for His voice. When the *Chief Shepherd* of the church speaks, the only adequate response is to *listen* and then *obey*.

I knew God was speaking when a local businessman by the name of K.C. Foster approached me. As K.C. opened up his heart and shared, I sensed that what I was hearing was more than just a *"good idea"*—it was a *"God idea."* He asked if the area pastors were praying together. We were not. In response, he gave to me a simple challenge that I believe was a word from the Lord—*Why don't you invite the pastors to start praying together?*

I wish I could say that the initial response to the invitation was an overwhelming success. It was not as it related to participation. In fact, for the first few years those who met for prayer were very few in number. If not for the conviction that this was God's idea and His encouragement through passages of Scripture like "Do not despise the day of small beginnings," and "He who began a good work will carry it to completion," we would have disbanded and went our separate ways.

But God is faithful. We started by meeting together for prayer once a month, but very quickly moved to praying every other week. Then we felt the Lord wanted us to pray on a weekly basis. We now pray every Tuesday over the lunch hour in a meeting room at the Elk River Public Library. God has added to our numbers! In addition to area pastors, there are a number of marketplace leaders who have joined us. Now anywhere from 12 to 20 of us meet for prayer each week.

And what do we do? The *atmosphere* of our gathering is *prayer*. When we walk through the threshold of the doorway we enter what we call our *prayer room*. Though the facility we meet in is a public facility, it has definitely been *sanctified* for a purpose. The purpose for our gathering is to meet God—to pray to Him, to worship and adore Him, to listen to Him and then respond to His leading.

In a group full of pastors and leaders, one may ask—who sets the agenda and leads the meeting? The leadership dynamic is unique in that there is a "facilitator," but his only role is to help facilitate discussion and to assist in keeping the group in a "spirit of prayer." A spirit of *mutual submission* has surfaced over the years. There's a high level of trust and mutual respect. As a group we are learning together what it means to submit to Jesus Christ. He is our leader. And we are becoming more sensitive to His leading through the person of the Holy Spirit.

As we continue to meet together, we are growing in our understanding that our unity has a definite purpose according to Jesus' prayer in John 17. We are moving from being *unified for the sake of unity* to being *unified for the advancement of God's kingdom* in our city. We are recognizing that God is calling us to work together to see our city reached for God. In prayer we are sensitive to His leading. God has been leading us to a number of *various initiatives* (you will be reading about them) that we can do together that promote unity and advances God's kingdom.

In short, our desire through the moving of the Holy Spirit is to be an answer to Jesus' prayer in John 17 when He poured out His heart to His Father for the Church's unity. We want to be an answer to our Lord's prayer.

CHAPTER 4
MARRIED TO THE LAND

BY PASTOR PAUL SALFRANK

My wife and I each wear *two wedding bands* on our ring fingers. Every once in awhile there are people who notice and ask about the *smaller one* that is right next to our wedding rings. We then tell them the story of how the Lord prompted us to *marry the land*. Allow me to explain what I mean.

In November of 1998 we had the opportunity to participate in a missions trip to Argentina. While in the coastal city of Mar del Plata, we were *learning* the principles of prayer evangelism by day in a conference and *doing* the principles at night in the neighborhoods of the city. During the conference I often thought of home (Elk River, Minnesota) and what God wanted me to take from what I was learning in Argentina back to my congregation and city .

I'll never forget one of the services I attended. The auditorium was filled with people who were hungry for God. The worship and teaching was anointed and God was doing a marvelous work in the hearts of His people. The mood was marked by exuberant celebration, and yet what I remember most was the "quiet work" God was doing in my heart. While others were standing and clapping and rejoicing, I was sitting quietly reading a passage of Scripture that I had read before, but it was different this time. It was one of those obscure passages that had a flashing "neon light" attached to it. I was drawn to it.

I sensed God by His Spirit speaking to me personally as I read from Isaiah 62, particularly verse 4. I know the prophet Isaiah was prophetically speaking about the city of Jerusalem, yet at that moment I sensed the Lord was directly speaking to me and what He was calling me to do.

Isaiah 62:4 reads,

> You shall no longer be termed Forsaken, Nor shall your land any more be termed Desolate; But you shall be called Hephzibah, and your land Beulah; For the LORD delights in you, And your land shall be married.

The flashing neon light was on the word *Beulah*. What does *Beulah* mean? The footnote in the margin read that *Beulah* means *married.* I sensed the Lord prompting me to *marry the land.* Not to marry the land that I was in at the time, but the land I was going back to, the land I call home. I chuckled to myself and wouldn't tell anyone because I didn't know exactly what it meant to *marry the land* and how you would ever go about doing it. I did share with my wife Deanna and we prayed about how we should respond to this word that we sensed was from God.

When we returned to Elk River, we asked the Lord for confirmation and clarification. God confirmed the word as we began to open up and share with others and God started to clarify what He wanted us to do.

First we were to go and purchase two wedding bands. We felt like a young engaged couple on a date looking and shopping for their engagement and wedding rings. We had a wonderful evening. We decided on a thin simple band, realizing that the most important thing was what the ring symbolized.

Our wedding rings symbolize the covenant we made when we looked into each other's eyes and spoke out loud our vows to love, cherish, and remain faithful and true to one another as long as we live. Similarly, the wearing of these rings would be symbolic of our covenant to God to fulfill the call He has upon our lives in the specific geographical area where we live. They would serve as a constant reminder that *we're married to the land.* The symbolism communicates commitment, dedication, and faithfulness. And just like in any marriage, through the good and hard times we desire to remain faithful to the covenant we have made to God to serve and help reach our city for Christ.

Secondly, we wrote down our vows and set a date to get married to the land. On December 5, 1998 in a gazebo in the center of town with a number of witnesses, we spoke out loud our vows to the Lord, placed the rings on each other's finger, prayed and were married to the land.

Prior to this marriage covenant our calling was primarily to our local congregation. We were called to build the local church that we served. But through the years God has been transforming our hearts and minds. We recognize that our calling is inseparably connected to and linked with the Church in the city. We know that it takes the whole church to reach the whole city, and to this larger calling we have pledged our lives. I'm often reminded of this covenant when I look down and see and feel the second ring on my finger.

CHAPTER 5

THE IMPORTANCE OF INTERCESSION

BY KEN & CARRIE BEAUDRY

We are the leaders of intercession for Pray Elk River. What does it take to bring a God-sent revival to a city? Does intercession play an important part in seeing revival in a city? Yes! Intercession is one of the key components to bringing revival and change to a city.

History has shown that to be true over and over again. Intercession is not always the thing talked about in a revival, but you will always find that there were faithful men and women of God who were praying for the very thing that God brought. We believe that by and through prayer, we can seek God for His plans and purposes for our city and then begin praying for what He has shown us, calling it forth and into being.

> ...God, who gives life to the dead and calls those things which do not exist as though they did. (Romans 4:17b)

> Behold, the former things have come to pass, And new things I declare; Before they spring forth I tell you of them. (Isaiah 42:9)

We view it as a circle of prayer. God reveals to us what He

is going to do. We pray it back to him, asking for it, calling and declaring it. It goes back to God and it is done. Then we thank Him for the answer!

Prayer by many groups

Many different groups have been praying in Elk River over the years. As a couple, we were involved in an intercession group that prayed every Friday night for a number of years. We prayed for a move of God generally and for youth specifically. Then a group of women from different churches felt led by God to pray for pastors and unity in the city. They prayed for a number of years. God was building relationships and unity of heart among a number of people from different congregations through different events in our city.

Spiritual mapping

The city was spiritually mapped and prayed for by a group of us under the leadership of Walter and Barbara Sukut. When we first started to pray, there was something like a poverty spirit over the city—spiritual poverty in the churches and an absence of youth groups, as well as financial poverty. Businesses had a hard time prospering and the whole business climate was undeveloped compared to other cities around us.

Changes begin

As we interceded, we began to see changes. Ministries started to come forth, businesses started to prosper, and land development began to thrive. The spiritual climate changed in about a ten-year period.

Intercession increases

In 1998, an Australian evangelist, Doug Stanton, held revival meetings in Elk River. During those meetings, God touched many people. We sensed an even greater need for intercession. We sensed that the Lord was calling us to lead a new intercessory group. As we began to pray, two passages of Scripture emerged as the foundation for this group. The first one was Isaiah 64:1-12, which focused our attention upon revival. We studied the story of the Hebrides Island revival, which confirmed this Scripture:

> [1] Oh, that You would rend the heavens! That You would come down! That the mountains might shake at Your presence—
>
> [2] As fire burns brushwood, As fire causes water to boil—To make Your name known to Your adversaries, *That* the nations may tremble at Your presence!
>
> [3] When You did awesome things *for which* we did not look, You came down, The mountains shook at Your presence.
>
> [4] For since the beginning of the world *Men* have not heard nor perceived by the ear, Nor has the eye seen any God besides You, Who acts for the one who waits for Him.
>
> [5] You meet him who rejoices and does righteousness, *Who* remembers You in Your ways. You are indeed angry, for we have sinned—In these ways we continue; And we need to be saved.
>
> [6] But we are all like an unclean *thing*, And all our righteousnesses *are* like filthy rags; We all fade as a leaf, And our iniquities, like the wind, Have taken us away.
>
> [7] And *there is* no one who calls on Your name, Who stirs himself up to take hold of You; For You have hidden Your face from us, And have consumed us because of our iniquities.
>
> [8] But now, O LORD, You *are* our Father; We *are* the clay, and You our potter; And all we *are* the work of Your hand.

> [9] Do not be furious, O LORD, Nor remember iniquity forever; Indeed, please look—we all *are* Your people!
> [10] Your holy cities are a wilderness, Zion is a wilderness, Jerusalem a desolation.
> [11] Our holy and beautiful temple, Where our fathers praised You, Is burned up with fire; And all our pleasant things are laid waste.
> [12] Will You restrain Yourself because of these *things*, O LORD? Will You hold Your peace, and afflict us very severely?

The second passage was John 17:21-22, where Jesus says,

> That they all may be one as you, Father, are in me, and I in you. That they also may be one in us, that the world may believe that you sent me. And the glory which you gave me, I have given them, that they may be one just as we are one.

From that point on, our goals were revival and unity. We went to pastors Bob Pullar and Paul Salfrank, who we joined in prayed once each week, and shared these two Scriptures with them. We covenanted with them to persevere in prayer until unity and revival came to our city. This was a three-way covenant between church, marketplace, and God.

For five years that intercession group continued to pray. We met every week, sometimes praying for three or four hours at a time. We worshiped the Lord and the Holy Spirit led us in this intercession. God gave us many prophetic words and visions and confirmations. We have prayed these things back to the Lord and declared, "It is going to happen, only believe it!"

God draws people to Elk River

We repented for current and past sins of our city. We did generational deliverance prayer for the city. We prayed specifically for each pastor and for each related congregation. Each intercessor fasted and prayed for their "adopted" pastor and congregation. We interceded for youth and we interceded for ministries. Youth ministries were birthed throughout the city. New youth ministers came to the city. People came to the city saying, "I am sent by God to the city." One pastor came from California who said, "I feel drawn to the city." Youth ministers came and said, "I feel drawn to the city." An evangelist came to the city saying, "I feel drawn to this city."

When we started praying, Elk River had one of the highest suicide rates in the nation. As we prayed against suicide, we discerned that there was a spirit of death over the city that led us to the history of Freemasonry in the city. We learned that Freemasonry brings a spirit of poverty and death. We also studied the Native American history in and around our city. God led us in intercession for this.

Things got worse before they got better

For a time, things actually worsened. There was a war going on for souls. Suicide even increased for a season. This was very discouraging. But eventually we turned the corner and the suicide rate dropped dramatically. In fact, the overall crime rate has now dropped by 25 percent.

Prayer in public places

We kept pressing in to God. We fasted and we prayed. God showed us what to do. We did prophetic acts. We prayed over various areas and intersections of the city.

One Sunday God showed us the four main gates to the

city. We took pastors and intercessors and went to these gates. We prayed and drove a stake into the ground at each gate. Each stake had verses of Scripture on it. We anointed each with oil and proclaimed the Lordship of Jesus Christ over it.

We also took part in intercession outside the city. Our "city intercessors" interceded at the Minnesota State Capitol.

God opened doors to us to pray inside each one of the schools in our city. We claimed each school, the students and teachers for Jesus Christ. We anointed each school with oil and drove a stake into the ground on each school campus. Each stake had Scripture written on it.

Fasting and prayer

During this time while we were interceding, only a few pastors were meeting together with the businessmen for prayer. Then God gave us a plan. He told us, "I want you to fast as Daniel did for 21 days." We organized different congregations to participate in this fast. Each congregation signed up 24 of their members with one person interceding and fasting during each hour for a 24-hour period. This was God's plan to bring unity among the pastors.

Then we saw the breakthrough. More pastors started praying together in the weekly pastors' prayer meetings. We began with two pastors, but grew to twelve pastors praying together. The pastors meet each Tuesday to pray from 12:00 to 1:00 P.M. As they prayed together, they began to love each other. The intercessors continued to pray for them and their fellowship kept growing.

Shift to pastor the city

Eventually, the pastors shifted their focus from pastoring their congregations to pastoring the city. The pastors now see that there is only one church in the city with many congregations. They have also come to recognize that it takes the whole church to take the whole gospel to the whole city. There is an amazing span of theological origins of these pastors. They come from Lutheran, Methodist, Nazarene, Baptist, Assembly of God, Christian and Missionary Alliance, Pentecostal and Charismatic congregations. Many denominations are coming together to serve the Master and to see His purposes come forth in the city.

City-wide outreach

One thing that was on our hearts was to see an evangelistic outreach where the gospel message would literally be brought to every home in the city. In 2003, the pastors decided to have an outreach called CAER and Share. CAER is the name of our local food shelf.

In the outreach, the city was mapped and divided up by streets. Over a thousand people from the different congregations participated. On one Saturday they went out to the homes that had been assigned to them. 9,000 homes or 99 percent of the homes in Elk River and Otsego were visited. Each resident was asked for a food item for the CAER food shelf. Each was given a copy of the *JESUS* video, which is a world-renowned evangelistic video. Each copy of the video ends with an invitation to accept Christ. Immediately within a week of this outreach, pastors were seeing results. After viewing the video, some people came to worship services on Sunday morning.

Worship

In this city, worship has been a large part of our intercession. For a number of years we did weekly or monthly community worship services. Our goal was simply to worship the King and to enthrone Him over our city. One of the words that God gave us was, "Make Elk River My throne room." We believe Jesus wants to be enthroned in this city through worship, so we never separated worship from intercession. Many people are writing new worship songs.

We sense a new sound coming from heaven. We've worshiped using some of these new songs. Then God called us to have the community worship and prayer in every congregation in Elk River that would allow us and He showed us that we were spiritually building the legs of His throne by doing this. Through all of this came the formation of Pray Elk River and Worship Elk River. These are alliances of the participating congregations.

Praying what is on Jesus' heart

Intercessors need to be totally in love with Jesus and to spend time with Him. One of our favorite expressions is "when we meet for intercession, we're not going there so much to pray, but to meet with Jesus." And if we kept that focus, there was no burnout. When we met on Tuesday nights, we would worship him, and then we would ask Jesus, "What is on Your heart? Jesus, show us what is on Your heart for the city tonight. Lord, what is burdening You? What is Your plan for us?" And He would always show up, and He would always give us direction. He was always faithful. Five years is a long time. We had spiritual authority in prayer because the pastors in unity in the city commissioned us to lead city-wide intercession.

We believe that each intercessor has to know who he or she is as the bride of Christ. If you want to see God move in your city, now is the time to start citywide intercession. Numbers are not that important at our intercessory meetings. We believe that two or three intercessors gathered together in the name of Jesus, out of their love for Jesus, can move the heavens over our city. This is simply a statement of our faith. Faith, believing the Word, believing who we are in Christ, believing that if our heart is right and we're coming together for the purpose of reaching the city for Christ, God will honor our prayers. So sometimes we had twenty intercessors, and sometimes we had three. It did not matter. God moved the same either way. We just persevered and did not look at the numbers. We looked at Him.

A Scripture has come to us recently over and over again. Jesus says in Matthew 18:19,

> Again I say to you that if two of you agree on earth concerning anything that they ask, it will be done for them by My Father in heaven.

Intercession changes a city

If you pray prayers of agreement, you will see things happen in your city. You will see God move. You will see that there will be angels all over the city doing God's work. You will see darkness destroyed, and the light of Christ rise in your city. You will see your governments change. We saw our government change. During the five years of intercession, God put a spirit-filled mayor in office. She would come to the Tuesday night intercession and pray with us. You will see congregations changed. You will see the marketplace changed. We are seeing more and more Christians rising up in the marketplace. The spiritual climate will change. Intercession will change a city.

God has a specific plan

God has a specific plan for your city, and He wants to show it to you. You can't take what someone else does in their city and say, "This is what we're going to do in our city." Everyone needs to seek the Lord and seek how He wants to redeem their city. Every city has a purpose. Elk River is a servant city. We are called not only as a city to serve, but also as a city to do intercession for other cities. So while we were interceding for the city, we were also planting seeds in other cities.

What is required is the gift of faith. That faith that rises up to believe for the impossible. That faith that rises up for you to grasp heaven—that God's kingdom would come on earth as it is in heaven. That was a common prayer, "God, let your kingdom come, let Your will be done in Elk River, as it is in heaven."

A prayer for you

We want to close with a prayer. We believe that as you pray this prayer, faith to see your city changed, will rise up within you. So please pray the following;

> Father God, I ask to see John 17:21-22 come to pass in my city. I agree with the prayer of Jesus for unity in my city. Father God, I desire to see revival within my city. Father, I desire to be an intercessor, to see intercession raised up to a new level in my city. Father, Your will is that none should perish, but that all would come to repentance. Father, I bow before You this day and humble myself before You and ask You to impart to me the gifts needed and the anointing needed to intercede on behalf of the city. Father, I ask now for the anointing to come. I ask for

impartation of faith. I ask for a measure of faith to be increased and released from heaven now upon me. Thank You, Father. I ask You for fresh anointing for intercession. I declare that there is a river that flows from the throne of God and of the Lamb and that river is here, and that river flows within me. Thank You, Father. I receive it in the name of Jesus Christ. Amen.

If you prayed that prayer, we believe that God gave you the desires of your heart. We believe that the Holy Spirit will take you to a new level.

CHAPTER 6
SCRIPTURAL FOUNDATIONS

BY PASTOR GREG PAGH

Two key passages of scripture have guided the movement of the Spirit called Pray Elk River. The first is Jesus' "high priestly prayer" in John 17. The second is Jesus' instructions to the seventy-two in Luke 10. The first provides the theological framework for God's call to greater unity in the church. The second provides a practical model for implementation through what has come to be known as Prayer Evangelism and the Lighthouse of Prayer ministry. While these are not new concepts, I want to share the impact these scriptures have had on our "city-reaching" efforts in the Greater Elk River Area.

Purpose in unity

Jesus' prayer in John 17 lifts up a huge vision for the Christian Church today. There he prayed for more than just his immediate disciples. He prayed for you and me, "...for all those who will believe in me through their message" (17:20b NIV). This prayer was offered the night before Jesus' crucifixion. Like a loving parent, Jesus poured out his heart for his children. Oh how it must grieve him today when we fall so far short of his desire for unity among believers.

When we zero in on chapter 17, verses 20-23, three main points describe the purpose of unity. **First, through our unity**

we become an answer to Jesus' prayer. I love it when Jesus answers my prayers, but what about being an answer to his prayers? Jesus' prayer is that both present-day believers and even future believers may be one, for the purpose of reaching the whole world for him. He says, "...that all of them may be one, Father, just as you are in me and I am in you. May they also be in us so that the world may believe that you have sent me" (vs. 21 NIV).

Certainly, if we as individual Christians and individual congregations are obedient to the Great Commission (Matthew 28) and the Great Commandment (Matthew 22), we will experience some success in our calling to serve the Lord. But to reach an entire city, to reach the whole world, will require a unified witness among the body of Christ that has yet to be achieved. That's what Jesus is praying for in these verses from John 17, and that's why I believe God is calling us to a new day of shared prayer and partnership in the mission of the church. Our purpose is not unity for the sake of unity. Our purpose is "so that the world may believe."

During the past six or seven years of shared vision and ministry, the Pray Elk River fellowship has kept this principle at the forefront of our work together. It's great that pastors and marketplace leaders gather to pray. It's a blessing that we are able to share in worship and activities that are beneficial to our communities. We enjoy our friendships, and quite frankly, the fun we're having working together. However, we are not interested in unity that merely serves our need for fellowship, or even peace between our congregations. Our God-given vision is that this whole city and the surrounding area will be reached for Jesus Christ. So, we always exhort one another to keep the eye on the prize. The purpose of our unity is transformation!

A second key point in this text is found in verse 22 and the first part of verse 23 (NIV). Jesus continues to pray, "I have given them the glory that you gave me, that they may be one as we are one: I in them and you in me." **Through our unity in Christ we reflect glory back to God and others.** In other words, the glory of God is given "to us" by Jesus to help us find unity, but it also becomes a witness "through us" for the world to see.

A great parallel passage to this principle is found in 2 Corinthians 3:17-18 (NIV). The Apostle Paul describes the glory of God this way. "Now the Lord is the Spirit, and where the Spirit of the Lord is, there is freedom. And we, who with unveiled faces all reflect the Lord's glory, are being transformed into his likeness with ever-increasing glory, which comes from the Lord, who is the Spirit." Once again we see the greater purpose of unity among believers. Jesus gives us his glory so that we can be transformed, becoming more and more like Him, and then reflecting His likeness to the world. It's like the power of a lighthouse. There is only one light, but that light is reflected through hundreds of lenses that radiate its glory. If our witness is to be powerful, we must stand together, and let the light of Christ shine through the whole people of God!

Our Pray Elk River fellowship has moved the churches in the area from a sense of competition to cooperation. It's not about individual glory. Our focus today is on allowing the glory of God to shine through the church of the city, again, so that the world may know that Jesus is Lord. When we drive by one another's churches, there is no cursing or suspicion. We know one another and we know the integrity of one another's ministries. Instead, we are praying prayers of blessing. This is the starting point for a real spiritual climate change in a city. Churches must catch a vision for a greater work of God than the success of their own congregation.

A third key in this text is found in verse 23b (NIV). Jesus prays, "May they be brought to complete unity to let the world know that you sent me and have loved them even as you have loved me." **Through our unity we mature into the fullness of Christ and give the world our most effective witness.** Complete unity means maturity, a fulfillment of God's purpose for us as Christians and for the church. Again, the Apostle Paul offers some wonderful words that build on this principle. He says, "Make every effort to keep the unity of the Spirit through the bond of peace" (Ephesians 4:3, NIV). Unity takes work. It's not our nature. Maturity is not a natural process. It's easier to stick with old attitudes and ideas, especially when they are so ingrained by years of seminary training and denominational indoctrination.

In our Pray Elk River fellowship we have worked hard for unity. We have not only prayed, we've talked, debated, listened, and learned to appreciate the different perspectives people bring. Unity does not necessarily mean uniformity. There are different gifts, and we have come to appreciate more than ever the diversity of God's family. What makes the effort worthwhile? It comes back again to our greater purpose. We are simply passionate about reaching a whole city for Jesus and being a catalyst for others to do the same. So we have accepted Jesus' challenge in John 17 to strive for "complete unity" to let the world know that we are not messing around. The day of the lone ranger is over!

Lighthouses of prayer

As far back as 1996, our Pray Elk River city-reaching efforts developed around what we came to understand as Prayer Evangelism. Luke 10:5-9 provided the foundational text from God's Word. We have continued to grow in our understanding of this simple passage and its practical application for how every Christian is called to be a Lighthouse of Prayer.

Two books by Ed Silvoso, the President of Harvest Evangelism, were instrumental in our understanding of these principles. *That None Should Perish,*[1] is based on Peter's exhortation in 2 Peter 3:9: God is "not willing that any should perish but that all should come to repentance." *Prayer Evangelism,*[2] delved more deeply into the paradigm shifts necessary to see the spiritual climate of an entire city changed.

We became convinced that a foundation of unified prayer among believers was the key to moving from evangelism by addition to evangelism by multiplication. Ed Silvoso is fond of saying we need to "talk to God about our neighbors before we talk to our neighbors about God." Prayer Evangelism isn't a program, it's a way of life. It involves reaching every person and bringing every household in touch with the power and love of God through prayer. That's something every believer is called to do and is capable of doing. Luke 10:5-9 provides a wonderful outline.

Speak peace and bless

As Jesus was giving marching orders to the seventy-two disciples he had appointed, he said, "When you enter a house, first say, 'Peace to this house.' If a man of peace is there, your peace will rest on him; if not it will return to you" (Luke 10:5-6, NIV). The first principle of Prayer Evangelism is to "speak peace to our neighbors." Our tendency is to curse nonbelievers and then wonder why they're not attracted to Christ. This was a huge revelation to me. Witnessing rightfully begins with prayer, but key to our prayers is a willingness to bless those around us.

Many of us began by walking our own neighborhoods and simply blessing, or speaking peace, upon the homes and families who were our next door neighbors. For others, "neighbor" meant those eight or ten co-workers with whom they shared an office. One of our high school girls decided to begin praying for the youth represented by the ten lockers closest to hers at school. When we pray in this way, something wonderful begins to happen. We begin to sense a change in our own hearts and attitudes. God uses these prayers to give us greater compassion for the lost and a deeper desire to take our concern to the next level.

Build relationships

In Luke 10:7 (NIV), Jesus continues, "Stay in that house, eating and drinking whatever they give you, for the worker deserves his wages. Do not move around from house to house." Here we see that Prayer Evangelism involves building relationships and sticking with people for the long haul. Sharing a meal, giving a ride, showing interest in another person's activities, and listening to their concerns are all ways of demonstrating the presence of Christ to others. Jesus was an expert at relational ministry. He met people right where they were at in life, and loved them in spite of their sin. To transform a whole city, believers must intentionally get out of their comfort zones and build relationships with nonbelievers. That often starts with those closest to us, our neighbors, co-workers, and classmates.

Discover felt needs and respond

Jesus continues, "When you enter a town and are welcomed,

eat what is set before you. Heal the sick who are there and tell them, 'The kingdom of God is near you'" (Luke 10:8-9 NIV). Two more important principles of Prayer Evangelism are revealed here. To "heal the sick," can be interpreted, "Discover a person's felt needs and respond to them." If a person is sick, really sick, not much else matters. Sometimes there is a deeper sickness that is not so easy to discern. The point is to minister to a person's felt needs first, so that over time their deeper needs can surface as well.

Declare the kingdom of God is near

I never miss an opportunity to pray with people today, but I start by asking them to tell me what they need prayer for. Nonbelievers love to tell you about their problems. (Don't we all!) I've learned not to stand in judgment, or to move so quickly to what I might perceive to be their real needs. I just offer to pray and let God go to work. When they begin to get answers for their prayers, believe me, their hearts are softened to the message of the Gospel.

That's when we are able to say, "The kingdom of God is near you!" In other words, "Jesus is real! He will not only answer my prayers for you, but He will answer yours! Wouldn't you like to learn more about a God who loves you that much?" One woman in her twenties said to me recently, "I've had questions about God my whole life, but nobody would listen. I really need to know if Jesus loves me!"

Prayer Evangelism follows this flow of speaking peace, building relationships, responding to felt needs, and sharing the Good News of Christ. The leading of the Holy Spirit is integral to the whole process. Remember, it's not a program. More than anything else, we want people to see the love of God at work in our lives and come to know that this same love is available to them. That takes time and a commitment to live out our faith in everyday life.

Those who implement this strategy of Prayer Evangelism have been called Lighthouses of Prayer. The Mission America network has summarized this teaching from Luke 10 with three wonderful words: PRAY, CARE, and SHARE! So many people have told me, "Pastor, for the first time in my life I have confidence in how to witness to my neighbors and friends. I can do this, and it works!"

In the fall of 2000, our Pray Elk River fellowship sponsored a "City-Reachers School" led by Ed Silvoso and his wonderful staff from Harvest Evangelism. That weekend we commissioned more than 500 families in our community as Lighthouses of Prayer and they went out one night and walked their neighborhoods speaking peace and blessing their neighbors. The weekend culminated with a giant Celebration of Unity service at the local high school with more than 2,500 people in attendance. The vision of Prayer Evangelism had caught fire in our community in a marvelous way.

You *are* a lighthouse of prayer

In the years since that time we have continued to emphasize the keys to Prayer Evangelism outlined above, but with one important change. No longer do we ask individuals and families if they would like to *be* a Lighthouse of Prayer. Instead, we remind them that they *are* one! In Matthew 5:14a, Jesus says, "You are the light of the world." The important question we must each ask is, "Are we letting the light of Christ shine through us to those around us?"

It is these two passages of scripture from John 17 and Luke 10 that have provided both the theological framework and the practical application for our Pray Elk River vision. We continue to call upon the Holy Spirit to help us press-in more fully to this revelation.

Our goals are simple. We want every person in our city to be prayed for by name, have a Christian friend respond to their needs in love, and have the opportunity to hear the Gospel and receive Jesus Christ. I just praise God when I see Christians from every walk of life embracing these principles and taking hold of the vision that some day soon we will live in a city that has been significantly transformed by the power of God in Jesus Christ!

Endnotes

1. Silvoso, Ed, *That None Should Perish,* Regal Books, Ventura, 1994
2. Silvoso, Ed, *Prayer Evangelism,* Regal Books, Ventura, 2000

CHAPTER 7
THE POWER OF UNIFIED PRAYER

BY PASTOR GREG PAGH

I am the Senior Pastor at Christ Lutheran, a congregation of the Evangelical Lutheran Church in America, located on the "other side" of the Mississippi River in the new community of Otsego, Minnesota. But more importantly, I am one of the pastors called by God to provide spiritual leadership to the "church of the city," not defined by buildings or denominations. It is this vision of unity and shared leadership in God's church that has captivated my heart and caused me to see beyond my own congregation.

I have not always been such an eager participant! When the concept of "city reaching" was first introduced to our Elk River Area Ministerial Association, it seemed strange and foreboding. As a Lutheran, I was not as familiar with some of the spiritual warfare language nor the potential for greater spiritual authority in a city through unified prayer. I read Ed Silvoso's book, *That None Should Perish*[1] with interest but did not grasp its immediate application for the Elk River area.

The invitation from K.C. Foster and Pastor Paul Salfrank and others to meet for additional prayer beyond our monthly meetings was welcomed. I loved these pastors, but time and time again my busy schedule (mostly self-inflicted) caused me to miss the noon prayer meetings at the public library. I guess my attitude was, "More prayer is never a bad thing, but for me it's just not the most important thing. I'm praying a lot already, and there are so many demands on my time in my own congregation. I'll get to this extracurricular activity when I can!"

My focus at this point in my life was clearly to build "my" church first, and then, if time permitted, contribute through prayer and various activities for the sake of the greater church in our community and beyond. It took a lot of love and patience from the other pastors, and most certainly the work of the Holy Spirit, to help me see the bigger picture.

Today this commitment to pray is at the top of my list! Only a rare emergency call will interrupt my attendance at our Tuesday noon prayer meetings. They are consistently one of the most blessed hours of my week. Why have my priorities changed so much? In short, over these years I have seen the power of God at work through unified prayer!

On a personal level, God has given me a bigger vision than the growth and success of my own congregation and/or the Lutheran denomination. I always knew this, philosophically or theologically, but I wasn't living it in practice. The Lord has convicted me of some self-centered attitudes that were not glorifying to God or contributing to the building up of the true body of Christ.

I believe that we have built our own fortresses of spirituality for too long. We've stood in judgment of the theology and practice of other Christians . We've settled for what I would describe as a "superficial ecumenism," content with profound theological statements and paper documents, but experiencing very little true fellowship with those outside our own religious circles. At our worst, we have criticized other pastors and congregations and made each other out to be the competition.

I believe that God is calling us to a new kind of unity in the Christian Church today. This true unity is birthed through prayer and bathed in the conviction that all who "name the name of Jesus" are brothers and sisters in Christ. Everything else is secondary. And here's the clincher. The work God is doing in His Church trumps anything you and I might think we're accomplishing in our own congregation or denomination. We need a bigger vision, and I have come to believe that it all begins with prayer.

We have a saying about each other now in the Elk River area. "We not only love one another, we like one another!" You see, we all know that in Christ we are supposed to love one another. Again, that's easy stuff on a theological level. It's like saying that you're in favor of world peace. But it's only as we have prayed together for years, shared our joys and struggles together over a meal or on a retreat and been in the trenches together working for the Gospel side-by-side that all the walls have come down. We can truly say that we like each other!

Today I am sold-out for these partners in ministry and the vision we share of seeing this whole area transformed by Jesus Christ. I speak well of these brothers and sisters and their congregations. I want to see them succeed for the sake of the whole body of Christ. They are not the competition! We are in this together!

Over the years, our noon prayer meetings have become a sanctuary for spiritual discernment, mutual support, and seeking God's direction regarding the vision of seeing a whole city reached for Christ. Many of the pastors and community leaders in our Pray Elk River fellowship would not consider making a major decision regarding their personal lives, ministries, or businesses without bringing their concern before the group for counsel and prayer. We have no elected leadership, and yet the spiritual authority resting on this group is unmistakable. Others in our community have recognized it as well.

Our prayer meetings have become a place for community leaders to share challenges and receive support and encouragement. Over the years we have welcomed leaders from government, law enforcement, education, business, and every other walk of life. We've prayed for mayors, U.S. Congressmen, our Secretary of State and Governor. We've "laid hands" on our Superintendent of Schools, school board members, principals and teachers.

Our Elk River Chief of Police, Sherburne County Sheriff, and personnel from the jail have sat in our prayer circle and experienced the power of unified prayer. Businessmen and women have shared their needs and received prayer support for faithful and ethical marketplace ministry.

God has blessed us in so many ways! A principal and his wife received healing from cancer. A school bond issue was passed. A drug bust was made. Many have come to the Lord in our county jail. Pastors have been "prayed-in" to our city. We've been able to encourage ministers and ministries of all kinds who want to be in the flow of God's Spirit and join us for prayer. And when there has been suffering and death, as was the case with our dear friend Pastor Dan Roelofs, we ponder the mysteries of God and continue to pray for grace and healing.

I believe that God is glorified through the prayers of His people. There is no doubt that the spiritual climate has changed in the greater Elk River area. There is an openness to spiritual things like never before. There is a hunger among many of the pastors and leaders to hear God's voice and be obedient to His calling upon our city. The hearts of the people are turning towards Jesus. We are convinced that we are on the verge of a tremendous revival where thousands will come to Christ and a fire will be lit that will spread to the Twin Cities, the State of Minnesota, the nation, and the world. Unified prayer is the launching pad for such a revival. God has promised to pour out a blessing when His children live together in unity!

> "How good and pleasant it is
> when brothers live together in unity!
> It is like precious oil poured on the head,
> running down on the beard,
> running down on Aaron's beard,
> down upon the collar of his robes.
> It is as if the dew of Hermon were falling on Mount Zion.
> For there the Lord bestows his blessing,
> even life forevermore."
> Psalm 133 (NIV)

Endnotes

1. Silvoso, Ed, *That None Should Perish,* Regal, Ventura, 1994

CHAPTER 8
A CHARISMATIC PERSPECTIVE

BY PASTOR BOB PULLAR

I am the pastor of a nondenominational Charismatic congregation within the church of Elk River and the surrounding communities. When presented with the opportunity to pray with other pastors in the community, I was faced with three undeniable truths. First, the charismatic wing of the church had often isolated itself from involvement with mainline denominations. Secondly, this gave room for misunderstandings and mistrust among churches. Thirdly, God was grieved! In the next few pages I would like to offer my perspective on these truths in the order I have stated them.

The isolation

It is not my intent to define why this isolation may have taken place (I suspect that all of us concerned liked it that way). I am very much aware that many men and women paid a high price to re-pioneer the liberty in the Holy Spirit that we now enjoy. I am also aware that this led to some broken relationships. To those who paid that price, I sincerely say, *Thank you!*

That being said, I clearly remember a day in my office holding a letter of invitation for unity in my hand and being convicted that Jesus Christ had paid a much higher price so that His Church might be unified. The Lord made it clear; I was called to the city, not just my local congregation. I recall being broken and making a heart-felt decision to work at helping to bring change. I was convinced I had a responsibility to begin to pray with pastors from the other churches in the community. I was without excuse and if I refused, God would be grieved!

Misunderstandings and mistrust

In obedience to the conviction the Lord had put in my heart, I began to meet for prayer with some of the other pastors. It was a bit awkward at first. I had a concern that I might accidentally offend one of my brothers. I felt the Lord had challenged me to "behave myself wisely." He exhorted me to focus on walking in the fruit of the Holy Spirit rather than the gifts. He taught me that the same Spirit that could cause me to move with boldness could also cause me to move with restraint.

I remember a prayer meeting when Gene Rick, the Methodist Pastor whom I have come to love and respect, announced that he was not accustomed to people walking around and praying so loudly. I informed him I was not accustomed to people praying so softly and only in English. We all laughed together. I realized that day that each of us was being stretched in one way or another. We were all allowing ourselves to be enlarged so as not to hinder what God was doing.

I do sometimes walk with my eyes open when I pray. I watch and I observe. I have observed men and women of God who love Him as deeply as I do. I have seen people in business, government and education that care about the spiritual future of our community. However, as I have encircled that room of bowed heads, I have never seen anyone with horns. I have been careful to sit with my head bowed that they might observe that I don't have horns either. We are a diverse group, but we all belong to Christ and we are His Church. We share the common burden of seeing our community changed by the Gospel of Jesus Christ. I may not understand or agree with their theology, but I understand their heart and I agree with their prayers!

Has it cost me something to join with my brothers and sisters each week for prayer? Yes, it has. It has cost me my time, my pride, my opinions, and my narrow view of Christ and His Church. However, it has not cost me my identity as a Charismatic pastor. Of all the pastors who meet together, I am the only one who has not been to a formal Bible School or College (I was trained in the local church). Over the years, the other pastors have never asked me to compromise who I am, but rather they have served to further validate God's call on my life.

I am not sure that I can say that we fully understand each other, but I sincerely believe we trust each other! I have a deep love and respect for those with whom I gather for prayer on Tuesdays. We have had services together, been on retreats together, and attended conferences together. We have laughed, we have cried, we have confessed, we have confronted, but most of all, we have loved one another!

God was grieved

I still remember that day in my office as I wrestled with the thought of joining other pastors for prayer. I felt my Father's displeasure at the hesitation in my heart. I do not know any other way to explain it except to say that I knew God was grieved. From that day on I have carried a sense of His brokenness over the disunity in His Body. From time to time I have felt compelled to ask my brothers for forgiveness for the part that the Charismatic stream has played in this disunity.

This book is about changing the spiritual climate over our

cities. I believe the first change that must take place in a city is to gain what Psalms 133 calls the "commanded blessing" of God. This comes from brothers dwelling in unity. We are not wise to set out to confront the powers of darkness if we are not walking in the light, nor can we find any lasting victory in breaking curses if we have not secured God's commanded blessing. This will only happen if leaders take the lead in establishing a genuine unity in a city.

I think most of us have found that our people have been very willing to follow *if* we will lead. In October of 2002, several of us pastors did a pulpit exchange on a Sunday morning. One of the ladies in my congregation was disappointed that the pastor scheduled to speak at our church was from a mainline denomination. She shared with me later that after she had heard him speak, she went to him to ask for his forgiveness for her prejudicial views. She was deeply impacted by the obvious call on his life and his love for God. I talked to that pastor sometime later. He was touched by her honesty. Most of all, I am convinced God was pleased!

Over the years we have seen a spiritual climate change. Most precious to us are the times when prayer meetings and community services are filled with a unique presence of God. I like to call that presence "the Father's pleasure." Those times leave a mark on us. It confirms to us we are on the right track.

We have been hesitant to write this story because we recognize there is much yet to be accomplished. The church of Elk River and the surrounding area has yet to take her rightful place in our communities. Nevertheless, we are a group of men and women who are co-laboring to fulfill the prayer of Jesus as recorded in John 17:21, "that they all may be one... that the world may believe that You sent Me." With *this* God is pleased!

CHAPTER 9
A New Pastor's Perspective

by Pastor Percy Kallevig

California is a lovely place. I had enjoyed ministering as an Assemblies of God youth pastor and senior pastor for 14 years in a beautiful climate. Nearly 10 years before coming back to Minnesota, I had enjoyed a Dallas Holm concert in Minneapolis. Out in the parking lot as I was about to leave I asked someone, "Where is Elk River, Minnesota?" They said, "Just down that road [Highway 10]." I felt God had spoken "Elk River" into my heart, but I never thought about that impression for the next 10 years.

A call to Elk River

In July 2000, I received a call from a board member looking for a pastor. I was ready to tell him I wasn't interested until I heard the words "Elk River." I said to myself, "Oh, no." I asked where the church building was located and the board member said, "We rent a storefront building." Again, I said to myself, "Oh, no." I had never in my life even attended a storefront church. Then I asked him how many were in church last Sunday, and he answered, "thirty-some." Another "Oh, no."

My wife, Debbie, and I came for a visit. We learned that Elk River Assembly of God had 25 acres of land to build a new church on in the future. The land was paid for; however, they didn't know how they would have the money to move us from

California should we be elected to pastor the church. All the while, God kept working on my heart and speaking to me.

100% approval

Another month went by and we came to candidate at the church. I preached in a morning service after which the members of the church would vote whether to hire us to pastor the church. While waiting for the vote to be taken and then counted I said to my wife, "Debbie, if I have one vote against me, I feel I can stay in California." She agreed with me, and we felt that if God really wanted us to come and if He had truly spoken to my heart to come, then that 100% vote would be there. When the board member came back to tell us the results he said, "Well, it was unanimous." Two months later, true to our agreement between God and us, we would be coming to Elk River, Minnesota.

A warm welcome into the city

After being elected , I went to the Tuesday Pray Elk River prayer meeting at the library from noon to one o'clock. The electricity in the air and the excitement as these local pastors began to pray for the city and then for me was an experience never to be forgotten. I was charged and ready to move!

Additional confirmation of God's work

I went back to my California church to resign. I was really sad and began clearing my desk of old junk mail when I noticed a letter from an acquaintance. I thought, *How did this letter get into that pile?* This was late August and the letter had been written in March. I read the letter written by a motherly Christian woman who did not attend our church, but did feel called to pray for us and encourage us.

The letter was what I expected: scriptures and praise reports. But there was also something I didn't expect. She wrote that she had a dream that I would be building a new church on rolling hills that were framed. I immediately called the board member in Elk River and asked him what "rolling hills" meant to him. He laughed and said, "That's our 25 acres, the church property; it's all rolling hills." As you stand on the property and look at it from the street, it is totally framed by trees.

We packed up, the moving van came, and we were on our way to Minnesota. Our house in California was sold but still not funded when we arrived in Minnesota. I prayed that God would get us into a home. God did get us a home the same week we got to Minnesota with no money down. The bachelor who owned the house was willing to move out in two days, and he was willing to wait for payment until our house in California closed escrow. He was also willing to rent us the house at a bargain price while he waited. What a blessing! Two months later, our home in California was sold and we completed the purchase of our new miracle home. We are still enjoying that home today.

Too busy not to pray

Right away, I believe because of God's prompting, I began to work on getting a new church building constructed on our land. After 24 months and many miracles later, we were in a new 10,000 square foot building. Through the process of building, I met with the Pray Elk River group. I was so busy that I really needed to pray and be with my city pastors. These pastors encouraged me and some sent checks - hundreds of dollars - to help us build. Have you ever heard of such a thing?

Sent to Africa by other pastors

When I came to Elk River in October 2001, I said from the pulpit that I desired to go to Africa in two years. During the two years from that time through the building process, since I was working as general contractor as well as preaching every Sunday, the thought of a trip to Africa had not crossed my mind.

The Pray Elk River pastors did not know of this desire when they asked me to go to Africa on a Vision trip to Rwanda. My internal response was that I'd love to go but that it took more money than I had. We had just finished a new building and I was sure all our resources were tapped. Where would the money come from? You guessed it! The Lord had provided most of the money from the Pray Elk River group — other pastors and churches helping this pastor realize a dream. When I went back to my church body and told them about the invitation, I didn't remember what I had said to my congregation two years earlier until one of my church members reminded me.

When I first became a minister, I had it in my heart to be able to build a church where one had never been before. That rolling hills acreage is now our church home. Our church finally has its own building. It took me until I was 47 to see it happen, and I'm 48 and going to Africa!

These two events and more came into reality because of a combined city effort of prayer, giving, and camaraderie among the church and business community of Elk River.

CHAPTER 10

Reclaiming Our Schools

BY CHUCK RIPKA

I am a marketplace Christian in the mortgage banking industry in Elk River, Otsego, and the surrounding communities. I am a member of the Christian and Missionary Alliance congregation that Paul Salfrank pastors. My Christian life has been filled with experiencing words of knowledge, wisdom, and prophecy. It has been tremendous for me to be part of this developing Elk River story with so many other pastors and marketplace Christians, and to watch Him maximize these gifts to help bring the kingdom of God to our city, county, and state.

I want to share with you how the Lord opened the doors of education to the riches of His kingdom.

The Lord gave me a vision in August of 1999 during a time of prayer. I saw two hands that were together bound with rope. And I asked the Lord, "Why are you showing me these hands?" He said to me, "This is how the teachers feel. They feel their hands are bound. I want you to go into the schools and tell the teachers that their hands may seem bound, but their voices are not bound. God wants you to begin to call Him back into the schools." Also the Lord told me, "I am doing a new thing. No longer will you pray on the outside of the schools, but now you will begin to pray on the inside. I want you to take back what has been stolen and reclaim the youth, the land, and the buildings for Me."

I asked the Lord, "How do you want me to do this?" He said, "Call the principal of the senior high, Jim Voight, and tell him that you want to meet with him." So I called Jim and asked if I could meet with him. As I met with Jim, I asked him if I could start a prayer group of teachers after school from 3:15 P.M. to 4:00 P.M. He said, "Well, how can I help you?" Will you put an announcement in the school bulletin requesting teachers to come together for prayer after school?" He said that he would.

I have learned that when I am obedient to what God has called me to do, there is no resistance. The doors are always wide open. That is what happened with Jim. Jim is a principal within the Elk River School District which educates about 10,000 kids. He was very open to this.

I said, "Lord, if this is truly You, give me at least one teacher who would respond." That is what I got - one teacher who responded,a few weeks later in September of 1999. We started the prayer group in October. While we started with one teacher, eventually we got as high as five teachers coming together, praying in the schools, praying for the students, praying for God to move through our schools. I gave that word again to the teachers, "The Lord knows how you feel, that your hands are bound but your voices are not bound, and it is time to call Me back into the schools."

Eventually I went into other junior high schools in the Elk River School District and we saw the same response. Teachers began to come together to pray and we began to see results. A math teacher came to the group and said that there was a student who was looking to quit school because work was too important. The student said that he couldn't work and go to school at the same time. So we prayed for that student. One week later that student came back to the teacher and said that he had quit his job saying that he had decided that going to school and graduating were the most important things for him to do.

On two occasions teachers were threatening to go on strike. We prayed for unity and the strikes were avoided.

Then the Lord said, "I want you to go into the schools and take back what has been stolen from Me." I said, "Lord, what do you mean?" He said, "The land, the buildings, and the youth have been stolen from Me. I want you to go into the schools and claim these things for Me." I responded, "Lord, how do you want me to do that?" He said, "Go to the school district and tell them that you want to start prayer walking the schools on the inside."

So I called the school district and said that I wanted to start prayer walking all of the schools in Elk River. Their response was, "The best time to do that is on Wednesday night. No one is there except for janitors." No resistance. They were even telling me when to do it.

The Lord showed me that I was entering into a new level of spiritual warfare. In warfare, when you take back land, you always post a flag letting the enemy know that you have taken back that land. The Lord said, "When you start prayer walking all the schools in Elk River, I will give you a Scripture and you will print that Scripture on a wooden stake (the Scripture would represent each school's identity and calling). After you are done prayer walking, go out to the school flag and pound that wooden stake into the ground. Then make a proclamation declaring that you have taken that school back for Me, letting the enemy know that you have taken that land away from him." Our mayor would come with us as well as teachers, students, and youth pastors. We would have anywhere from 25 to 50 of us going into the schools. That began in the Spring of 2000. Throughout 2000 we prayer walked each of the schools - elementary schools, junior high schools, and senior high schools. We had powerful, powerful evenings of prayer.

Then in September of 2000, Ed Silvoso came to Elk River. And at a Mayor's prayer breakfast, Ed asked me to pray for the schools. I had never prayed publicly before. I asked the Lord how He wanted me to pray. He said, "Chuck, I want you to pray for the referendum. It has failed for the last two years in a row, but I am going to see that it passes this year."

So I got up in front of all of these city leaders and told them that the Lord is going to get the referendum passed this year because the physical conditions of our schools represent the spiritual conditions. I told them, "God says, 'I am going to pass the referendum to restore the physical assigned to you. And He is going to restore the spiritual also.'" Then I prayed and I sat down.

After that breakfast meeting, David Flannery, Superintendent of Schools, approached me and said, "Thank you so much for praying for the schools." After we had shaken hands the Lord said to me, "A new door has just opened to you." So I left and said to the Lord, "I sense that you want me to pray with the Superintendent of the school district. When?" He said, "Tonight!" I got anxious and nervous and responded, "Can't we wait for a month or so? Shouldn't I pray more about this? Why tonight?" He said, "I have things that I want done right now." And I said, "Okay, Lord, if this is truly You speaking to me, I will call David right now. One, he has to be there. Two, he has to take my phone call. Three, he needs to be receptive to this. And Lord, I am busy tonight, but I have 8:30 P.M. available."

So I called David at lunchtime. Of course he was in and took my phone call. I said "David, the Lord just spoke to me." And this is one thing that I really like about the Lord, He allows me to speak to people as the Lord speaks to me, and people always continue to receive it. I told the superintendent that the Lord just spoke to me and he didn't question it. I told David, "The Lord just told me that there is unfinished prayer that needs to take place tonight in the school. David, can you join me tonight, in prayer, in the school?" He responded, "Well, Chuck, I have two meetings tonight, one at 6:00 P.M. and one at 7:00 PM. I can be there at 8:30 PM." I said, "That's perfect. I'll see you there tonight."

Ed Silvoso was at our church that evening doing a radio broadcast with the pastors. They all prayed over me and sent me off to pray with David Flannery. Ed Silvoso gave me a word saying, "Chuck, I see you leading a tidal wave through the schools of Elk River. You will lead a tidal wave of students. I just see you taking over the schools. Revival's coming."

That confirmed to me that more things are getting ready to happen in the Elk River schools. As I was walking across the street to the Elk River High School, I was still anxious. I said, "Why do you continue to do this, Lord? I am not comfortable doing this. But you know that I won't say no." The Lord replied, "Chuck, I know that you will go." I said, "Yes, Lord, I will go, but I'm not happy about it. I am physically feeling anxious about this because You won't tell me what is going to happen until I get there.

I got to the school and David Flannery was there. Here we were, just the two of us, the superintendent and me, in the senior high school at 8:30 PM. David said, "Okay, Chuck, what do you want?" I thought, "Okay, Lord, you are on." Immediately the Lord told me what to say. "David, we're two men on a mission. You are after the physical reconditioning of the schools, and I am after the spiritual reconditioning of the schools. He replied, "Don't get me wrong, Chuck, we want the spiritual here also." So I replied, "Perfect, then we need to pray. David, if you will lift Him up then He will lift you up. And He is going to show the nation what He can do when He gets a hold of a school." And David said, "Chuck, I want that." So I said, "Let's join hands and pray."

As we joined hands the Lord stopped me and said, "Chuck, you can not pray with this man yet. This man has been cursed. The city has cursed him. The city has cursed his family. The city has cursed the schools. The city has cursed the students. You can not pray with this man with dirty hands. You represent the city of Elk River. You need to repent on behalf of the city and break the curses that have been spoken against him." So I said to David, "Before I can pray I need to repent and ask forgiveness because we have cursed you, and your wife, and your children and your home, and the schools and the students." I broke the curses that had been spoken against him and he forgave us. And then the Lord said, "Now you can pray." I began to invite Jesus Christ into the schools, along with the superintendent.

I got done praying and I asked David what *he* would like to pray. He said, "Chuck, I don't pray like you pray." But he said, "I am going to pray for you personally that the Lord would continue to use you in the schools. We need people like you."

We prayed for that referendum in September. Between that time and the election, the newspapers were predicting that the referendum would fail once again. In November, they held the election and the $108 million referendum passed (because the Lord said that He would pass it). This was the biggest news in Elk River that year.

Then thirteen months later, the Lord told me to pray with Alan Jensen, the new Superintendent of Schools. I came to know Alan and to pray with him. We brought together the Mayors of Zimmerman and Elk River, the Superintendent, the principals of the schools, the director of the school board, one of the members of the city council of Elk River, many pastors and youth pastors, the Chief of Police, and the Sheriff of Sherburne County. Just a year earlier it had just been David Flannery and I praying for the schools. Now we had a little over 100 people gathered to pray for the schools.

This time we had two hours of prayer and testimony. At the very end we prayed for the Superintendent and the school board. Once again the Lord told me to repent for relying upon the schools to raise our children. All of us repented to the leaders of the school system. We declared that it is our job to raise our children and it is the teachers job to teach them.

When Ed Silvoso was in town in 2000, about 50 of us went into the high school in the afternoon and we did a prayer walk there. I went up to the janitor and explained what we were doing. I explained that we were doing the same thing that he is doing. He is cleaning the school physically, and we are cleaning the school spiritually. Then we prayed over the hands of the janitor and anointed his hands with oil. Now he not only can do the physical cleaning, but also the spiritual cleaning.

Janitors will often direct us to where the strongholds exist in the school.

There was one time when we prayed over another janitor. I was about to leave and somebody asked me if I had led that janitor to the Lord. I was convicted that I did not ask the janitor if he wanted to receive Christ. I went back in the building and I told the Lord that if I would meet the janitor when I returned into the building, I would take this as a sign that I should lead him to the Lord. I did encounter that janitor on the way back into the school. When I asked him if he would like to accept the Lord, he said yes and allowed me to lead him in a prayer. Then he asked me if I would pray for other feltneeds in his life.

One of the reasons that I went into the schools was because of the epidemic of suicides that occurred in Elk River. Now after four years, because so much prayer has been sown into the schools, the number of suicides has dropped dramatically.

CHAPTER 11
MOBILIZING THE YOUTH

BY TOM NESS

When I started as Youth Pastor at Christ Lutheran Church four and one half years ago I knew I wanted to find support, encouragement and fellowship with others who were ministering to youth in our community. I found that in Allies—Elk River, a network of youth pastors from the Elk River area. The network had been meeting for several years and had a history of doing large community wide events together. During my first year at Christ Lutheran we did a few events together and met monthly, but we also saw some turnover in the youth leaders in the area.

In the fall of 2000 we worked together to bring Milton Creagh into our schools for a school assembly followed by an evening program where we shared the Gospel. We were blown away by the number of youth that returned to hear Milton Creagh speak at our evening program. Over 800 youth showed up and over 100 youth made a commitment to Jesus Christ that night.

Planning and praying for this event brought us together as a network and reminded us that God is in control. It wasn't us that brought over 800 youth back that night—it was a God thing. We continued to plan events together over the next three years. They ranged from another Milton Creagh school assembly with a parents meeting at night, to Pre-See You At The Pole Rallies, to an alternative Halloween party, to monthly worship services held at churches, to other fellowship events. These events have had various purposes but the one constant has been a continued challenge to Christian students to see themselves as missionaries to their school.

Personally, the events we've done as a network have been a benefit to our individual youth ministries, but I believe the real strength of our network has been the relationships and connections that have developed between youth pastors, youth, congregations and even the community. Praying together and sharing with each other has brought a sense of unity and shared mission.

Through these connections, we have seen the power of prayer as youth leaders from different denominations unite with a common goal. The schools of the area have opened their door to allow the pastors of the area to come and minister.

Every Wednesday, we enter the public schools during the student's lunch break. Youth from many area congregations and their friends gather around and talk with the youth pastors. This has brought about a spirit of unity among the Christian youth in the community. One girl made the comment, "It's easier to hang out with Christians from other congregations because we see you hang out together."

They are indeed seeing themselves as Christians with the same mission of reaching their friends. For instance, during the past four years various ministries have started and been run by students. For a year a worship service, called the Burn Service, was planned and led by youth in the high school auditorium. It was a place where youth came together to worship and pray for their friends and school. They saw themselves as missionaries to their school. In addition, a group of youth started a Tuesday morning Bible study being held at the high school. The unity among Christian youth has enabled it to grow and be sustained over the past four years. It is led and attended by youth from various churches. Many youth also say it is an easy place to bring their unchurched friends because it is located on their school campus.

God has also used the time at the lunchroom on Wednesdays in other ways. One Wednesday, a youth pastor was brought in by an area youth to lead a suicide prevention meeting. Through this encounter, he was able to share God's love with the hurting youth. The school counselor in this meeting also happened to be a Christian and expressed her desire to connect with the youth pastors in the future. God is bringing connections across multiple lines for a common purpose: to reach the youth for Christ.

There is definitely an environment of cooperation between the schools and youth pastors. This past fall when a new high school opened in our district the youth ministries in our areas were invited in by the principal for a service of dedication and blessing on the new school. Christian teachers are able to support and encourage Christian students.

The youth are not the only ones benefiting from these times together. It gives the pastors of the city support and encouragement. We share ideas, resources and most importantly prayer together. We do a better job of keeping youth from falling through the cracks because of our relationships and we are able to do a much better job of ministering to all youth.

Last year, a girl from another congregation joined one of our small groups with a friend. I was able to tell her pastor that she was plugged in to a small group through our congregation. Because we have a sense of unity and a knowing that we're all part of one team, he was glad that she was being ministered to. He didn't have to worry that she was falling through the cracks but instead knew she was connected and growing. This year she is back plugged into her own congregation. The communication and sense of unity allowed us to minister to her as a team.

Another example of our sense of being on the same team occurred when a ministry from outside of the area called congregations in the area to find a good fit for a particular girl moving into the area. She described the girl and the style of ministry she was looking for and three different congregations all pointed to the same particular congregation in the area. The girl is now plugged into this congregation. Again, it is only because of our sense of unity that this kind of cooperation can happen.

Additionally, we've found a place of support and encouragement as pastors ministering to youth. We are able to be a resource for each other and to share ideas. The youth ministries in this area are connected and healthy. We hope this enables us to keep the same youth leaders longer and with a common vision of reaching youth together.

There is definitely a unity among the youth pastors in our area. It started with meeting to plan an event together, but it has grown into much more. The times of sharing together and praying for each other have turned us into a team that cheers for each other and supports each other. And it has spread to the youth as well.

CHAPTER 12

A Mayor's Perspective

BY MAYOR STEPHANIE KLINZING

Now firmly entrenched in the service of the Lord, I knew I was being called to run for election to the open seat of mayor of Elk River. In my spirit I could feel the tugging. I could feel the excitement, but I could also feel an apprehension.

Two things were at the root of this. Having been out of public office for four years following a six-year stint—four years as a county board member and two in the State House of Representatives—I couldn't imagine why the Lord wanted me to return to dealing with the world's issues when I had just started working in various areas of ministry. Also, my family and my business—writing church history books—kept me very busy, satisfied, and happy.

Yet I knew that this calling would mean so much more than being in a decision-making position over city issues. I knew that the Lord would never ask me to do anything that would not include His issues. Somewhere in all those discussions about roads, land zones, taxes, and budgets, He would be there.

My spiritual sense of great things to come began early in the campaign in the spring of 1998. I could feel something building in Elk River that would attract national and possibly international attention. I remember telling my friend in Christ, Rosie Elizondo, that I could see television personality Geraldo Rivera coming to Elk River to see "what was going on." In my vision, Geraldo asked, "Why are you doing these things?" We in Elk River shrugged our shoulders in stunned amazement at this question saying, "We are only doing what seems natural to us."

Another confirmation of my calling to become mayor of Elk River came when a stranger—whom I later came to know was Chuck Ripka—approached me in the grocery store one day and told me that he was praying for me because the Lord was calling me to this office. Throughout the campaign I was confident that the Lord had everything in His will. If He wanted me to be elected I would be and if He did not want this, I wouldn't be elected. It really made no difference to me. I simply wanted to follow His will.

Although I worked very hard during the campaign door knocking, making personal appearances, and attending debates, I balked at one event which I knew the Lord was asking me to arrange. In my other campaigns for public office, I had participated in "literature drops." These events are very labor intensive. They involve gathering a large group of volunteers who spend a day distributing campaign literature door to door. I hated organizing these "drops" and hated even more participating in them. But I could sense the Lord urging me to make arrangements for a "drop" and I even went as far as setting a date for the event and getting the volunteer notification cards printed. However, I hesitated and did not mail the cards.

One day in the parking lot of St. Andrew's Catholic Church, my friend Dr. David Gilgenbach approached me and said that he had received a word from the Lord for me during

Mass. He was a little reluctant to speak the word since it didn't have any meaning for him. Because he has a prophetic gift, however, he knows when the Lord wants a word delivered. The message was very simply "get on with it." I started laughing as soon as I heard those words. I told David that I knew exactly what the Lord wanted and I also thanked him for being obedient. I sent the cards out that day.

The day prior to the scheduled "drop" another friend called saying that he wasn't available on the scheduled day, but could take some time the day before to drop literature in the city. I delivered my friend a bundle of campaign literature and sent him on his way. Much later that day I talked to his mother-in-law who said that my friend had not returned home yet after being out all day. Later that evening I talked to him to inquire about the reason for his delayed return home. He explained that behind every door was someone who wanted to talk about the candidate—so he spent all day talking about me.

My friend's witness about his experience raised questions in my mind about the procedure he was using to deliver the literature. He explained that he would got to a house, knock on the door, and then when someone would come to the door, he would hand them the literature and spend time talking about the candidate he was supporting. I informed him that he had not operated under the usual "drop and run" rules of a literature drop, but had actually gone "door-knocking" for me. As it turned out, my friend's efforts probably added the winning touch to my campaign since I won by only 60 votes, which was about the number of homes he had visited that day.

My election as mayor of Elk River came with much celebration of the faith community. There was a general sense that the Lord was up to something. And what a *something* it continues to be!

Prayer became a major part of my service to the city. I asked for prayer and prayer was also being offered for me by individuals, groups, and churches who had received the word from the Lord. I attended a Sunday service at Living Waters church just prior to the National Day of Prayer in 1999 and ended up as one of a small group praying for our country. As we sat hand-in-hand with heads bowed, the woman holding my right hand started praying for the mayor of Elk River. She offered a wonderful prayer asking the Lord to lead me and protect me and my family. After we were done praying and she saw whose hand she was holding, she exclaimed loudly, "It's you!" She informed me that she prays for me every day. What a blessing that was!

For the first time in my public career I began seeing the Lord's hand in everything with which I dealt. This was a result of prayer—mine and that of the faithful in Elk River. When a difficult situation was slated to come before the city council, I would go to the Lord and take authority over it in the name of Jesus. The entire atmosphere of the meeting would change and everything would go much easier with a high level of peace. People would still express their frustration, but no amount of anger or hatred would be raised during the meeting.

I came to realize that with my position as mayor I also have a spiritual authority as the political head of the city. I have used this authority to keep out things I felt would have been harmful to the city and invite in things that I believe the Lord wanted brought into the city. I became acquainted with the pastors of most of the churches in Elk River through my association with Pray Elk River. I began to attend the Tuesday noon prayer meetings and join them in prayer and seeking the Lord's will on the advancement of the Kingdom in Elk River and the surrounding area. I learned that Pray Elk River had been born out of a desire to see Elk River reached for Jesus Christ. Harvest Evangelism representative Rick Heeren, and his former colleagues, Eric Straub, and David Sluka, assisted Pray Elk River in forming the framework through which the work of evangelizing the entire area would be done.

During my first two years as mayor I witnessed a growth among the pastors of Pray Elk River; both in numbers, influence and spirituality. I attended several day-long retreats along with the pastors and businessmen as we sought a closer relationship with each other and clearer direction from God. A servant leader team was chosen and given the authority to lead Pray Elk River.

In October of 2000, Pray Elk River, in conjunction with Harvest Evangelism, sponsored a week of evangelical outreach events in the city. Included was the first Elk River Prayer Breakfast. This breakfast provided an excellent opportunity for me to discuss my faith in a "public" forum for the first time. The second opportunity came only a few days later when Pray Elk River held a community-wide service in Elk River High School gymnasium. Attended by a crowd of over 2,000 people, representing every church in Elk River, I was able to publicly express my faith in Jesus Christ and proclaim that Elk River would be a beacon to the world of the saving grace of our Lord and Savior.

Proceeds from the collection taken up at the community service were presented to me as the mayor of Elk River. I pledged to use it for the benefit of needy Elk River citizens.

Hence the Mayor's Samaritan Fund was started with $15,600.

The community service received front-page coverage in the Elk River Star News the following week. Included in the information about the service was a direct quote from the mayor of Elk River expressing her belief in Jesus Christ and the city's existence as a beacon for the saving grace of our Lord and Savior.

When I read the article, my public office experience told me to prepare for a very large backlash from citizens critical of my taking a public stance on my faith. But I immediately put it into the Lord's hands. If He wanted to protect me from the critics, He would. If He felt that it would be good for me to feel the sting of criticism, so be it.

The subsequent silence was amazing. No irate telephone calls. No critical letters to the editor. Nothing! I realized that God had given me a supernatural favor with my constituents and a protection from arrows of criticism that could bruise even my tough political skin. I did not earn nor do I deserve this favor and protection. They are a gift. I am constantly aware of what great gifts they are. There is no doubt that I am freer to be who I am as a follower of Jesus Christ because of those gifts.

There is now doubt that the week-long evangelical movement in October of 2000 catapulted Elk River into a higher spiritual dimension. At the weekly Pray Elk River meetings, the prayer was more intense and directed. Also, the prayer intercessors, who were meeting weekly at Beaudry Oil offices, were experiencing greater intensity in their prayer for the city.

I also sensed a greater unity among the members of the Body of Christ in Elk River. Interdenominational prayer teams were sent out to cover in prayer every point in the city—schools, businesses, government buildings, transportation routes, residential neighborhoods, and natural waterways. The core group of prayer intercessors also did extensive spiritual mapping of the city and surrounding area and then targeted those areas that the Lord was indicating needed to be reconciled through prayer.

The highlight of this time of intensified prayer was the revelation that we needed to begin to operate as "the Church of Elk River" instead of being Christians from such and such church. When I first heard this word, I knew it was extremely significant. The Lord led me to focus on John's account of the Last Supper when Jesus prayed "that they all may be one..." (John 17:21a).

This word from the Lord came at the perfect time. We were ready to accept where God was leading. We had come to see in each other a genuine love for the Lord Jesus Christ and because of this, we had come to love each other. The pastors began to understand that they needed to move outside the walls of their churches to pastor the city. Denominational barriers began to fall away. Our love and acceptance of one another was firmly routed in our mutual love for Jesus and nothing else mattered any longer.

We continue to walk in that unity today. Very little evangelical outreach is done in Elk River outside of that unity. The Lord has shown us that there is power in what we do as the Church of Elk River and that there is no limit to what can be accomplished when the Body of Christ moves in unity. In Jesus' own words, "That they may be made perfect in one ..." (John 17:23b).

CHAPTER 13
A Week That Changed the City

BY RICK HEEREN

This chapter relates the chronological activities that took place between, August 22, 2000 and October 1, 2000. This exercise was based on what Ed Silvoso, in his booklet, *My City, God's City,* called a Prayer Evangelism Launch.

August 22, 2000 - Congregational Board Members meeting
This was a gathering at Central Lutheran Church in Elk River of participating pastors and their board members. The main purpose of this meeting was to brief the board members on the Biblical principles of prayer evangelism and to prepare them for the upcoming prayer evangelism launch, beginning on Friday, September 22, 2000. The majority of those board members agreed to support their pastors as they committed their congregations to this process.

September 22, 2000 – Mayor's Prayer Breakfast
This was the first ever Mayor's Prayer Breakfast to be held for the people of Elk River. It was held at Riverwoods Inn in Otsego, MN, which is right next to Elk River. Mayor Stephanie Klinzing presided over this breakfast meeting and Ed Silvoso was the main speaker. During the breakfast, Ed Silvoso asked businessman, Chuck Ripka, to pray for the schools in Elk River. This prayer led to a divine encounter between Chuck and

David Flannery, who at the time was Superintendent of Schools in the area. You can read about that encounter in Chapter 9, Reclaiming our Schools, by Chuck Ripka.

September 22, 2000 – Morning meeting between Harvest Evangelism staff and the pastors of Pray Elk River, at Christ Lutheran in Otsego

During this half-day gathering, the pastors of Pray Elk River prayed over the staff of Harvest Evangelism, welcoming them into the area and commissioning them to minister. This gathering also included fellowship and lunch.

September 22, 2000 – Afternoon Marketplace Seminar at Christ Lutheran in Otsego

This was a forerunner of what became known as the Anointed For Business Seminar.

September 22, 2000 – City Reachers Welcome Dinner, at Christ Lutheran in Otsego

This was an opportunity for out-of-town visitors to meet with the staff of Harvest Evangelism and to learn more about the process of reaching cities for Christ through prayer evangelism.

September 23, 2000 – City Reachers School, at Central Lutheran Church in Elk River

This seminar covered a full day on Saturday, and included Ed Silvoso teaching about the Biblical principles of reaching cities for Christ through prayer evangelism.

September 24, 2000 – Morning preaching by Harvest Evangelism staff at each of the various congregations participating in Pray Elk River

All of the Harvest Evangelism staff preached the same message about Luke 10. At the end of each service, each Harvest staff member passed out cards so that congregational members could sign up to be a Lighthouse of Prayer. After the services all of the Harvest staff had lunch together at Chuck and Kathi Ripka's house and tallied up the number of Lighthouses of Prayer that had been launched that morning. There were about 500.

September 24, 2000 – Evening City Wide Celebration of Unity, at Central Lutheran Church in Elk River

Ed Silvoso led this united worship and prayer service. This celebration of unity was a moment of declaration and commitment to shepherd the city.

September 24, 2000 – Evening City Wide Celebration of Unity for the youth in Elk River

September 25, 2000 – Morning prayer at schools by youth

September 25, 2000 – Evening Lighthouse of Prayer Radio Broadcast

In this broadcast the pastors and the Harvest Evangelism staff led Pray Elk River members to dedicate their homes as embassies of the kingdom of God in their neighborhoods. This radio broadcast established points of light all across the city.

September 26, 2000 – Morning prayer at schools by youth

September 26, 2000 – Evening Lighthouse of Prayer Radio Broadcast

In this broadcast the pastors and the Harvest Evangelism staff led Pray Elk River members in prayers to sanctify their hearts and their homes. Through this radio broadcast a spirit of sanctification came upon the city.

September 26, 2000 – Evening outreach to youth

This was led by Milton Creagh and the youth pastors of Elk River and the surrounding communities. 800 youth attended and 100 made public decisions to accept Christ.

September 27, 2000 – Morning prayer at schools by youth

September 27, 2000 – Evening Lighthouse of Prayer Radio Broadcast

On this date we sent Lighthouses of Prayer into their neighborhoods with portable radios to pray peace and blessings, according to Luke 10:5, over their neighbors. Through this radio broadcast, the Church occupied the land as we prayer walked the entire city.

September 28–29, 2000 – Strategic intercession throughout the area

September 30, 2000 – Door-to-door visitation to distribute invitations to the prayer fair

October 1, 2000 – Morning united worship services at Elk River High School

The pastors closed their congregational meetings and 2,500 people gathered together in the gymnasium at Elk River High School. Ed Silvoso preached about Luke 10 and more Lighthouses of Prayer were launched. An offering of $15,600 was given to Mayor Stephanie Klinzing in the name of the City of Elk River.

October 1, 2000 – Afternoon Prayer Fair

The prayer fair was set up in Lyon's Park in Elk River. Through this prayer fair, the Church of Elk River went public with its commitment to pastor the city. The various congregations established booths for praying for the "felt needs" of those who attended the prayer fair. For instance, if a person showed up and said that they needed prayer for physical healing, that person was directed to the booth that was staffed by those who had an anointing to pray for physical healing. If the person had a financial problem, that person was directed to the booth that was staffed by those who had an anointing to pray for financial miracles. Also, people with marital problems were directed to the booth that was staffed by persons with an anointing to pray for the healing of marriages.

CHAPTER 14
THE SHERBURNE COUNTY JAIL

BY REV. JAY BUNKER

I pastored a church in Elk River for 35 years. I am greatly blessed to see the answer to many years of prayer and fasting for this community. Since I retired, my wife and I find it very rewarding to minister in the jail. We see the fruit of our labors almost weekly. We also travel and minister in many churches in the U.S., Canada, Mexico, and on many Indian reservations. We see the stirrings of revival everywhere!

Our ministry at the jail is a branch of Pilot Outreach. This organization is a nondenominational group of men and women volunteers that provide bible studies, prayer, and spiritual counsel for the prisoners. This group ministers at many of the local county jails, as well as a Sheriff's Ranch for troubled youth.

There are two chaplains who are ambassadors for us, and we are under their authority, as well as the jail staff. The men volunteers have four weekly Bible studies that are conducted on Tuesdays with the male inmates. Women volunteers also meet weekly for a Bible study with the women inmates. On Sunday evenings, we conduct five concurrent worship services in the jail. All services and studies are held in meeting rooms. I am one of forty-three volunteers who go into the jail on a weekly basis. Twelve of us are authorized for professional one-on-one visits. Sherburne County Jail is unique for it is not just a county jail. It is a holding facility for Federal, State, and B.I.C.E. (Bureau Immigration Customs Enforcement) inmates.

The Body of Christ in the jail is by its nature a transient group of people. There are not many that spend longer than one year there. Inmates are free to have their own Bible studies on a daily or weekly basis. They choose the person who will lead their groups and we give them advice on what to study.

We have many heartwarming accounts of men and women whose lives have been miraculously transformed. What a joy it is to watch them become grounded in Christ and His Word, as they receive Bible studies and discipleship instruction. Since many people are not county inmates, they leave Elk River very quickly and go to another facility, or back to their own county. We always hear good reports from many nations as these men and women live and share Jesus in their corner of the globe.

A few years back a local businessman had a vision of Christ being rooted into Elk River. Many churchgoers in the area were in agreement with this vision. So a day to pray for Elk River was set. On this day many area Christians marched and prayed for local homes, churches, businesses, and government buildings. By permission, the jail was included in this march. As we marched, we proclaimed a spiritual awakening for each establishment.

The spiritual awakening that is now in its early stages includes the Sherburne County Jail, which is located in Elk River. Currently there are about 360 men and women being detained in the Sherburne County Jail, and there are plans for expansion. Approximately 100 of those inmates come to our weekly services. We pray daily that God would increase that number. The United States currently has about 1.9 million people incarcerated. This is more than any other nation. We think that this is a field ripe for the harvest, and believe for a greater harvest of souls.

CHAPTER 15
EXPANDING MARKETPLACE PARTICIPATION

BY KEN BEAUDRY

I am a marketplace Christian in the wholesale and retail oil industry. Just as a newly found oil field in the ground has untapped and unlimited wealth in the oil industry, so does the marketplace have unlimited potential, vision and resources for winning our cities for Christ. We are in the process of awakening the marketplace to this calling.

My story about the marketplace begins in 1988 when my cousin, Mel Beaudry and I, saw the need for men to come to Christ. We started to pray one hour a week and soon K.C. Foster joined us. This was the start of a journey for three of us who wanted to see men changed in Elk River. We met each Wednesday at noon for one hour. God continued to bring new people to our group.

For ten years we ministered to a multitude of men. In 1998, through people such as Rich Marshall, Ed Silvoso, and Rick Heeren, God started to show us that there is a calling on each marketplace Christian. He showed us that each marketplace Christian in our city can play a role in ministry. He also showed us that Jesus' first disciples were taken from the marketplace. Then He showed us that throughout history God has used marketplace Christians to accomplish His work on earth. We now see how marketplace Christians can become Lighthouses of Prayer to their community. We also see that they can be spiritual leaders to their employees. Our vision was beginning to expand.

Imagine a city where every professional, every truck driver, every delivery person, every business owner is in love with Jesus and knows that their profession is their calling. This is our vision for Elk River. It will happen one person at a time.

In Elk River, businesses are being transformed, taking on new vision and purpose in Christ. In Luke 19:8, after Zacchaeus met Jesus, he was transformed and gave half of his wealth to the poor. We have seen this kind of transformation happening in Elk River.

Elk River had a history as a ministry graveyard, a place where it seemed almost impossible to get ministries started. It used to be a city where you couldn't raise funds to accomplish God's work. There was a spirit of poverty over the city, even though many wealthy people lived here. That is now changing. I believe prayer is a vital part to seeing the marketplace transformed.

In the last four years we've seen multiple ministries start up in Elk River. Priority Associates, a ministry of Campus Crusade for Christ that ministers to businessmen, has brought a ministry to our area. Timber Bay Youth Investment, a ministry that ministers to at-risk kids with the help of businessmen and churches, now has a full-time staff person in Elk River. Businessmen, with local churches, founded a ministry called Love Elk River, a ministry that reaches out and responds to the physical, emotional, and spiritual needs of the residents in the Elk River area. A Boys and Girls Club chapter was brought into the area, and YMCA is interested in coming to our city. These are just a few of the signs of a move of God in the marketplace of our city.

Over the years we've seen countless men and women in the marketplace ask for prayer. We've sent teams out to businesses to do "spiritual cleansing" and to pray for prosperity for these businesses. One of the most fascinating things for me is the answered prayer from our Lord for financial needs. I can honestly say I've seen God move more profoundly in this area than in any other area in my life. Time and time again, when a group of business people come together to pray for a fellow businessperson, we've seen incredible financial miracles.

The stories are many over the years, stories like that of a computer support specialist who started his own business and came from another city asking for prayer because there was no business. In the weeks after we prayed for him, he had so much business he couldn't keep up with it all. Another is of a man who was fired from a bank executive position and came for prayer and direction. Over the following years he ended up as part owner and CEO of a bank. At the personal level, my company has tremendously prospered because of the prayer of my fellow business people. Countless times, I needed favor from God with a customer or have needed finances to make ends meet. These prayers have always been answered.

Not only are business people coming to our city for prayer, but there are those who are making God the foundation of their business. Recently, a bank opened up in our sister city of Otsego. The bank is founded by a group of Christians, and its policies are based on Christian principles. On the cornerstone of the building is imprinted, "In God We Trust". Much prayer went into the forming of this bank with a special dedication to Christ. After the bank opened, many salvations were reported. Also, the bank CEO's wife, who was suffering from a back ailment, received prayer and was healed. It's not uncommon for people to go to this bank to get a loan and end up receiving prayer or salvation.

This is our vision for the entire city, that businesses would become places of ministry, and that the church would be in the marketplace. As CEO of our oil company, I have people come to my office on a regular basis to receive prayer for healing and deliverance. There was a local trucking firm that was being harassed by a large customer of theirs, and after prayer, the harassment stopped. Another company had family divisions and fighting, and after the businessmen prayed, unity came to the family. Another man who was a salesman for a lumberyard asked for prayer for direction. After much prayer by his other marketplace Christians, he is now a successful builder.

In our city we have a local chiropractor that plays Christian music on his office sound system and prays for his clients as he works. We have a convenience store owner who goes to the jails and ministers and prays for the inmates on a weekly basis. There is a manufacturing VP/owner leading a Bible study at his office. A real estate agent prays for his clients.

We all help each other, and as we have given, we have received, and all of us have prospered beyond what we could dream or expect from God. We have insurance agents, real estate salespeople, mortgage bankers, retailers, wholesalers, all of whom are some of the top people in their field, and we all say it is God! We've seen God take businesses in Elk River and the surrounding area and use these businesses like bullets in His gun to shoot down poverty and lack and provide funds to further His kingdom.

Of course, in this respect the evil one knows the potential of businesses that are dedicated to Jesus Christ and the furthering of the Gospel. We have seen a need for increased prayer to continue the prosperity and peace that God intended. At Beaudry Oil Company, we've tried to be a model of this, we now have on staff an intercessor who prays an hour a week for our company, customers and employees. Any concerns I have, I take to our intercessor. The president of our company and myself meet each week to pray for the company and concerns. My wife has led Bible studies for employees. Also, a mortgage bank has put an intercessor on staff to pray for their bank, plus there are countless owners and CEOs praying for their companies. This, I believe, is only the beginning of what God wants to do through the ministry in the marketplace.

As the marketplace in Elk River becomes more and more dedicated to Christian principles and lifestyles, the effect that our local marketplace will have on our city, county, state, country and world will become more and more evident.

What can one city do? It's absolutely astounding what God can do with the marketplace in one city. As an example, over the last couple of years, we've had marketplace people taking incredible leadership. Two businesses sponsored an evangelistic outreach for high school kids that saw many come to Christ. One local mortgage broker led intercession groups to our State Capitol for multiple prayer meetings and brought mayors from all over the state together for a prayer summit. He also led intercession teams to local schools to reclaim the schools for Christ. A local trucking operation hauled relief supplies to impoverished people. Multiple marketplace associates are traveling out of our city in ever increasing numbers to Mexico, Barbados, Jamaica, Haiti, Ukraine, Argentina, Peru and China, to name just a few, to build shelters and homes, do evangelistic outreaches, build churches, supply vehicles, and to provide food in soup kitchens and prisons.

We declare and continue to declare that this is only the beginning - that His kingdom will come on earth as it is in heaven.

CHAPTER 16
RIVERVIEW COMMUNITY BANK

BY CHUCK RIPKA

The Lord told me in 2000 that Duane Kropuenske and I were supposed to begin a new bank. Duane told me, "Chuck, you know a lot about mortgage banking, but you don't know much about running a bank. I want to mentor you in general banking so that you can take over the bank when I retire." I responded to him, "Duane, the Lord just spoke to me and said that as you mentor me in the things of banking, I am to mentor you in the things of the Lord." Duane and his wife, Patsy, agreed and together we have grown a great deal over these last three years.

We had to raise $5.5 million in capital in 2002, and in March 2003 we officially opened the bank. During that process, I prayed that the Lord would cause a stirring about who should invest in this bank. There were three groups who said that they were going to invest, but the Lord gave me a check in my spirit about receiving their money. I prayed that the Lord would cause these three groups to decide not to invest, and in each case they did not invest. Of the 48 investors, 30 of them are local business people.

Two weeks before the bank opened up, I prayed about what should go on the cornerstone of the bank. Then the Lord told me to put these words on the cornerstone, "In God We

Trust." The week before the bank opened up the Lord told me to pastor the bank. "Take what I have taught you and pass it on to others," He said. "Teach others within the bank to pray for the customers. Not only will your customers make physical deposits into your bank but you will also make spiritual deposits into your customers." Then the Lord began to draw customers into our bank.

The Lord told me, "Chuck, if you will do the things I've called you to do, I will take care of the bottom line." Within the first 9 1/2 months, we reached our 3-year goal of business. Our initial goal was to reach $15 million in deposits in those 9 1/2 months—we actually recorded $43 million. By the end of 2003 we had led 45 people to the Lord. That includes 7 employees, 3 of their spouses and the rest are customers and a few waitresses at local restaurants while we were in lunch meetings.

Also, during the Fall of 2003, I brought a healing minister, Ian Andrews, to the bank and set him up to pray in our boardroom. During that ministry time, 19 out of 21 employees, and a few customers, came into the boardroom for prayer. A large majority received their healing immediately.

The Lord said, "I am going to cause such an acceleration of this bank, that you will be invited to speak to secular groups about what has made the bank successful." I had a vision of business people in the audience listening to me telling them how the Lord has guided us in the development of this bank. Even as this story is being written, it is beginning to happen.

CHAPTER 17
LOVE ELK RIVER

BY MAYOR STEPHANIE KLINZING

On October 1, 2000, at a citywide service uniting seven congregations in the Elk River area, the faith community took an offering and gave me a check payable to the City of Elk River for $15,600. I then designated the funds to help those with needs in the community, establishing the Mayor's Samaritan Fund.

God began to raise up and bring in people who could benefit from the fund. No one had to advertise it or make it further known. People were simply "sent" to the administrators of the fund. This evolved into a formal ministry, under the authority and covering of Pray Elk River, a group of united community pastors. Named Love Elk River, the ministry is the hands and feet of Pray Elk River. Love Elk River was designed after the ministry model instituted by Jesus in Luke 10, when He sent out 70 followers two-by-two into the communities where He would soon visit. Their primary mission: to announce that the Kingdom of God is at hand.

Love Elk River was formally established in 2002 and several members of the Elk River area faith community were invited to serve on a governing board. The original expressed description of Love Elk River was that it is a relationship-based network of support, administered by united members of the greater "church of Elk River" who are passionately in love with following the will of God and devoted to the demolition of denominational barriers and walls.

During the first few months of meetings, the Love Elk River board members struggled with understanding God's intended purpose for Love Elk River. As board chair, I have led the group to seek the Lord's wisdom through prayer about the mission of Love Elk River. We have begun to see Love Elk River specifically commissioned to shepherd people whom God is calling "out of darkness into His marvelous light" (1 Peter 2:9c) for His purposes so they could take their God-designed place in the Body of Christ to advance the Kingdom of God. (Also see Ephesians 5:8; Acts 26:18; 2 Corinthians 4:3-6.)

Here is what the Lord has given us as His mission: to do whatever the Lord is asking for those He is calling out of darkness into His marvelous light for His purposes. We have prayed to the Lord of the Harvest for laborers and we believe that the people raised up to Love Elk River will become those laborers. Love Elk River is not a general assistance ministry. We are specifically called by God to specialize in finding, raising up, and sending out those people God is calling into the harvest field as laborers. He is calling them from the highways and the byways and they are down-and-out, beat up, and dragged out. But God has put a call on their lives. They are the ones who have been through the battles and know the enemy. They have great promise to be dynamos in the Lord's work.

The underlying truth by which Love Elk River is guided is that every person referred to Love Elk River is rich in spiritual inheritance through Jesus Christ and is being called by God for His purposes. Therefore, everything done for people referred to Love Elk River by counselors, ministries or social services (or by word of mouth) serves to unveil that purpose through the internal workings of the Holy Spirit in that person's life.

Love Elk River is neither a branch of social services, nor a community "gap-filler," nor a church recruitment outreach. In fact, God has shown Himself faithful to stop the action of the ministry team if it begins to use money, time, resources, etc. in ways that are out of His will and timing. The life situations encountered by Love Elk River ministers are often impossible situations with seemingly no solutions.

The team members are trained to die to their own first impressions and judgments. Situations of great need must be constantly put into God's hand. There is always "more" that could be done, but the Love Elk River team may or may not be the one to do it. Obedience is crucial. Because of this Love Elk River does not always bring comfort. More often than not, the sin nature of the person referred to Love Elk River is exposed, and the person is dealt with personally by the Lord. Spirit-led friendship and support are more important than material help at this time. God designs even their trials to bring them to the place where they are able to follow Him. Sometimes He even instructs a team to walk away, so that He can deal with the person in a different way.

Experience has shown that walking in God's will and grace prevents caregiver burnout, frustrations and defeat and keeps the recipients from becoming dependent and demanding. Every step of the ministry points to Jesus Christ as the source of all goodness.

The most important quality for one who would minister with Love Elk River is that they be a lover of unity and of God's will above their own. Because of the relationship base of its ministry, involvement in Love Elk River is a serious, long-term covenant commitment. The actual amount of time commitment varies from time to time, depending on the number of people who are being discipled.

When a needy person is identified, a team of three or four is called upon to pray together, discern the present need and the desires of God, and go into Spirit-led action, using their own God-given gifts. Their job is to impart hope to people who are in hopeless, messy situations. God calls them in from the highways and byways, people who have "fallen through the cracks" and are in the outer darkness. Each precious soul has a call on his or her life for a special purpose, and God is using Love Elk River to call it forth.

Love Elk River trains people to serve on its ministry teams. These people are referred to as "intercessors" and are required to go through a discernment process in order to identify if they are being called by the Lord to become involved in the ministry. Intercessors are also required to sign a certificate committing themselves to the work of Love Elk River. The certificates must also be signed by someone identified as the person's "spiritual director." This is necessary because of the need for the person to be under a spiritual authority in order to resist the enemy.

All Love Elk River intercessors must also be members of a church or faith community. Intercessors serve in several capacities within the ministry. Some will go out during visits (divine appointments) with a team, others are ministry leaders, others are observers, and others stay behind and intercede for the teams as they go. Without intercessory prayer backup, the visiting teams, who many times encounter sensitive and even dangerous situations, will not be effective. Prayer cover is essential.

There are other intercessors who carry the burden for each recipient of ministry—on an ongoing basis. The enemy will be on the attack once these precious ones begin to come into their God-given purpose and destiny. They need to have their armor reinforced by the faithful prayers of God's intercessors.

Love Elk River does not have a pot of money on-hand for financial and materials needs which intercessors discern the Lord intends to meet for ministry recipients; nor does it seek to build a pot. According to Luke 10, the disciples were told to bring nothing with them and not even a bag to gather things as they went. Resources for God's work through Love Elk River come through a "call network." This network is made up of people, groups, and businesses who have agreed to be notified whenever a resource need is identified and that prayer discernment has determined God intends to meet for someone who has been raised up to Love Elk River. The call is sent out and those in the call network go to the Lord for His wisdom on whether or not they are being called to meet this need and to what extent. This keeps every aspect of Love Elk River before the Lord and keeps the ministry moving in His will only.

Love Elk River has also heard and is answering an urging from the Lord to establish emergency and transitional housing opportunity in and around Elk River. Currently the ministry has one house being used as a site for a transitional housing program and another house is slated to be available in May of 2004. These houses are leased, for a minimal charge, from the City of Elk River to Love Elk River and then a local church mission group administers the transitional program in the houses. The mission group has all responsibility for the program, the property, and the family selected to participate, who are either homeless or in danger of being homeless. Transitional housing is available to the family for up to two years. During the time they are in the program every barrier to the family qualifying for permanent housing is addressed. This is a life-changing experience for the participating families, who are constantly surrounded by God's people throughout their stay in the transitional program and Love Elk River houses.

"Thanksgiving House welcomes family for Christmas" was the heading of an article in the local newspaper in November of 2002 highlighting the opening of the transitional house to its first family. The City of Elk River had approached Love Elk River the summer of 2002 about leasing a three-bedroom home owned by the City and using it for transitional housing.

During my term in the Minnesota House of Representatives, I worked on the subject of emergency housing. Based upon this background, I was excited that Love Elk River could assist the community in this manner. River of Life Church agreed to serve as property managers and take the lead in providing support to the families living in the home. They and many others, including several businesses and organizations in the Elk River area, worked hard to get the home ready.

The first family excitedly took residence just before Christmas of 2002. The following was written in a thank you note from the family given to Transitional Housing Manager Herb Langer at River of Life church: "We would like to thank you all for the things you gave to us, the Christmas gifts, the tree, the wonderful Christmas dinner was had because of all of you. It is wonderful to be able to shower and sleep and not have to worry all night long wondering if you're going to be the only one alive in the morning [their trailer had a gas leak problem]. The house is a beautiful place and we love it. But the greatest gift all three of us got this year was finding out that in a world where things are going so bad, so fast, there are still people who really do know how to love, and how to show it. We thank you very much for all you've done."

Love Elk River is also exploring the purchase of a multi-family apartment building, a motel, and mobile homes to be used for emergency and transitional housing. These properties will extend Love Elk River's relationship-based network of support ministry to include housing where recipients can be supported in a more stabilized situation.

Again the idea is not to just supply someone who is needy with a place to live but, more importantly, to surround them with God's people doing His work of calling them out of darkness into His marvelous light for His purposes. Love Elk River is exploring various avenues of funding for the housing, including private and government sources.

Here is a quote that I gave recently, "We believe that Love Elk River will be a model that can be used all over the country. I am excited that the fund that was started in October of 2000 can be continued and expanded. It is having a great impact on people's lives."

There is a sense of anticipation and restlessness in the hearts of people involved with Love Elk River. It is as if they know they are on the verge of something big—only they do not know what it is! There is change in the air. God is moving in Elk River! From here, the ministry of love will go out into all the earth.

We are forerunners. We have something very special and unique to accomplish in this area. We are right in the center of a giant jewel which God is bringing to His bride. It is our time to shine. Let us awake, as from a long sleep, and go out to meet Him as we say *yes* to Him in whatever He asks.

CHAPTER 18

WORSHIP ELK RIVER

BY PAM KRINGLUND AND DEBBIE DELONG

Worship Elk River is a group of worship directors from our area that have been meeting on a regular basis since May 2001. Debbie DeLong and I have been vice-chair and chair of Worship Elk River and together we are writing our story.

The Pray Elk River group of pastors was planning our second citywide community service for July 2001. It was to be held at the local fairgrounds on a Sunday morning, and participating churches would be encouraging their parishioners to attend this special service. My pastor, Paul Salfrank of Alliance Community Church, approached me about making the arrangements for the worship portion of the service; the pastors would be working on the rest. As I agreed to his request, I immediately knew how to accomplish this - I would contact the worship directors from the participating churches and together we would work out the details.

This similar strategy had been used successfully nine months earlier for a Harvest Evangelism conference that culminated with our first community service. We had needed a number of community worship teams for those events, and several of us had sat down and put teams together, drawing from our own individual teams. So, with this strategy in mind, I put out the invitation to the Pray Elk River churches for their worship directors to meet with me to plan and coordinate the worship for our Fairgrounds Service.

Our first meeting went well, with nine participants. As we put a team together, we discussed the possibility of future meetings to share ideas as worship directors. I asked about worship workshops in particular; I had been researching them for my own team. (Deb and I had talked about this prior to our meeting, and we were excited about the prospect of jointly doing something.)

Out of that discussion, we all agreed in concept it would be great fun to corporately put together a worship workshop for our churches, yet something that would be open to other area churches. So, as we continued to work on the fairgrounds service, we began to plan and strategize for a community workshop that we could tailor to suit our own needs, and one that would be affordable and accessible as well.

Plans for the Fairground Service went smoothly. It was such a joy working with the other directors, taking a rather large task and breaking it into bite-size pieces. Everyone had something to contribute, even if it was just ideas. We contacted Dan and Sandy Adler from Heart of the City to lead worship (they'd done the first community service), provided the additional musicians and singers for them, organized a community choir from our churches, coordinated the practices, made arrangements for the stage and choir risers, worked with the sound company, located banners to be used for the service, and provided refreshments since everyone would be arriving early that morning.

What a wonderful sense of God's approval and pleasure we experienced as we began our worship that beautiful sunny Sunday morning. It was exhilarating to see our pastors, joined by our mayor, worshipping together on our makeshift stage as people poured into the stands. What a significant time spiritually for Elk River! Just as our first community service had been so anointed and powerful, this too was no disappointment.

With that task behind us, we worship directors began to work with diligence on our first Community Worship Workshop to be held the end of September. God was so gracious in inspiring and guiding us - we excitedly put all the pieces together. It was during this process that we sensed direction from the Lord to "officially" organize into a group, a group that would not only sponsor this upcoming worship workshop, but could sponsor and coordinate other events as well in addition to providing support for the Pray Elk River pastors.

We also looked forward to opportunities to share and pray with one another as part of our purpose for meeting. So with that, we became "Worship! Elk River" with the Pray Elk River pastors providing our spiritual covering. Our mission statement reads, "Worship Elk River is a group of area worship directors, in partnership with Pray Elk River, committed to enriching the expression of worship in the Greater Elk River Church." At times we have expanded that concept to embrace evangelism and church unity. However, in its briefest form, this is the mission we believe the Lord has given us.

Our first worship workshop was entitled, "Experiencing the River"; we thought that theme was especially prophetic for Elk River. We were led to draw primarily from our local resources for worship and teaching. Classes were offered in two tracks: technical and topical. Technical classes were for dance, flags, musicians and singers, sound and a round table discussion with pastors and worship directors. Topical classes included blended worship, intimacy with God, and of course, "experiencing the river." Pamela Nelson from St. Cloud and her band lead us in worship at the close of our workshop. It was so exciting to see people come together from area churches to learn and grow. The teaching and worship were outstanding, and we received very positive feedback. The benefits were on many levels; people were individually blessed as they participated, and again The Church was brought together and unity strengthened.

Our next sponsored event was "An Evening with Andre Ashby" who is gifted in prophetic song. There was a great turnout for this. Andre shared in prophetic song, "Get ready! The King is coming to Elk River!" This reminded us of many other prophecies we have received for our community. "Let the wells spring forth of the presence of the Lord. Let the river flow!"

We know worship will play a key role in the coming revival. We were then onto another worship workshop scheduled for March 2002. We felt we were to sponsor worship workshops once a year in the spring, so we pressed into the Lord for direction for what was to become an annual event. We were so blessed when Dan and Kelly Willard agreed to come and help. The theme the Lord gave us was "The Heart of Worship" and we knew the Lord was going to use Kelly to show us the heart of a worshipper!

We again used many gifted instructors from our area, and just like the first workshop, the Lord blessed it tremendously. Titled classes were "Foolishly lavish worship," "The heart of worship," and a Biblical study on "What happens when we worship." Additional classes on leading children in worship, and the worship arts, in addition to the standard classes for worship leaders, singers, musicians and sound were offered.

As Kelly led worship both Friday night and Saturday afternoon, we clearly sensed great peace and the powerful healing presence of the Lord. It was a very precious time for us. One of the weekend highlights was the processional on Saturday afternoon to the song "The Heart of Worship." What a moving experience!

After that project, we again sought the Lord for His will concerning us. Following a time of prayer, we began to get a vision for a Labor Day event held in our local park and band shell that would include a variety of talent from our churches. As the event began unfolding, we saw God use this to reach out to other area churches since every church was invited to not only attend but participate. Again, God was using us to help build unity in The Church.

The Lord worked numerous miracles for us, such as providing a sound company that donated their services for the entire day (which meant they began setting up the night before, worked all day into the evening, and tore down that evening and next morning)! Our "Labor Day Family Fun Fest" included two separate tents for prayer and children's activities, an information table for area churches, concessions by several church ministries, and various "acts" in the band shell ranging from clowns to readings to music groups. We culminated the day with forty-five minutes of community worship and sang, "God bless America" as one community choir member held an American flag the Lord had told her to bring. Once again, God was honored and we were blessed!

Since Labor Day, we have provided worship teams for a 9/11 Memorial Service and a Community Prayer Service held in our new Elk River Senior High theatre. We are currently working on our upcoming annual Worship Workshop to be held the end of February. The theme this year is "Passionate Worship".

We have recently changed our meeting format to allow us to do less business and more fellowship and prayer. We're excited about the possibilities this presents. For example, we'll be watching a portion of a *Transformations* video at our next meeting. Surprisingly, none of us have seen them. More of our business will be taken care of in committees, and this should be more efficient. We will continue to meet once a month over lunch. Prayer has played a key role in everything we've done - we pray and He directs! Then our goal is to bathe everything we do in prayer, asking God for His will to be done, and we encourage everyone participating to intercede with us.

We have a strong sense of the importance of our roles individually as well as corporately, knowing that worship will be a major component of revival in the Elk River area. Many other events have paved the way for our Worship Elk River group, specifically two different series of revival meetings, ladies ministry at Alliance Community Church that gave birth to the beginning of community worship and prayer services, and preparation for that first community service held in October 2000.

Strong relationships have been built through working together on various worship services, and our community worship and prayer services have continued in some form or another for six years now. We have even used each other's musicians at times when we were short-handed at our own churches!

We have been blessed beyond words as we've watched God move in our community. It is so clearly the hand of God in response to all of our prayers. What an honor and privilege it is to play a role in what He is doing. We give God all the glory, knowing it has been "not by power, nor by might, but by the Spirit of God" that He has raised us up for "such a time as this." We look forward with anticipation to what He has in store!! Maranatha.

CHAPTER 19
A CITY DETONATING PRAYER EVANGELISM

BY RICK HEEREN

Elk River is now a working prototype of prayer evangelism within the Twin Cities Metroplex. This prototype has proven that the principles of prayer evangelism taken from Luke 10:1-9 really can change the spiritual climate in a city. We are now seeing groups of pastors and marketplace leaders from other cities being influenced by the Elk River prototype.

Anoka County, Minnesota

Pastor Jarry Cole, then with Abundant Life Church in Blaine, MN, participated actively in the process during 1999 and 2000, whereby the Pray Elk River pastors accelerated the implementation of Prayer Evangelism. During this same period, Pastor Greg Pagh, of Christ Lutheran Church (in the City of Otsego), contacted his friend Pastor Blair Anderson at Lord of Life Lutheran Church (in the City of Ramsey), and shared some testimonies about what was happening in Elk River and Otsego.

After participating in the meetings in Elk River, Pastor Cole communicated the Elk River testimony to Pastor Ted Nordlund, then of Anoka Covenant Church (in the City of Anoka), and Pastor Blair Anderson of Lord of Life Lutheran

Church (in the City of Ramsey) and encouraged them to join him in arranging a meeting with pastors and marketplace leaders throughout Anoka County. Anoka County is immediately to the east of Elk River.

A breakfast meeting was arranged at Lord of Life Lutheran Church in Ramsey. The mayor, four pastors and three businessmen made a presentation about their positive experiences with prayer evangelism in Elk River and the surrounding communities. Based upon that testimony, the leaders of Anoka County have committed to join with Harvest Evangelism to implement prayer evangelism within their county. Pastor Randy Discher of Constance Evangelical Free Church (in the City of Andover), Pastor Blair Anderson of Lord of Life Lutheran Church (in the City of Ramsey), and Pastor Tom Stuart of Bridgewood Christian Church (in the City of Blaine) are currently providing leadership to that project.

Bemidji, MN

The pastors of Bemidji were planning to do an area-wide evangelistic outreach, entitled *Rise Up America*. They called me and asked me if I would come to Bemidji and make a presentation encouraging participation in their event. I declined based on the fact that our ministry is not focused upon events, but rather upon ongoing processes of implementing prayer evangelism in order to reach cities for Christ.

Shortly after declining, I received a telephone call from Pastor Steve Thompson of Mt. Zion Church (in the City of Bemidji). He said that even though he had never met me, he was overcome by a feeling of sadness when he heard that I had declined. He urged me to reconsider. Shortly after that, I was at a pastors' gathering with Pastor Don Pfotenhauer of Way of the Cross Church (in the City of Blaine, MN). Pastor

Don and Pastor Steve had been communicating about this subject, and Pastor Don urged me to reconsider the invitation from Bemidji. Based on this input, I contacted Pastor Steve and told him that I had reconsidered and would be glad to serve the pastors in his area regarding the promotion of their event. I also asked him if it would be possible to speak with those pastors about the idea of implementing prayer evangelism in Bemidji after they had finished with their event. Pastor Steve agreed.

After the *Rise Up America* event was over, Pastor Steve invited me to make a presentation to about forty pastors from Bemidji and the surrounding communities. I told those pastors about the way that the leaders in Elk River had joined us in implementing prayer evangelism. They were very interested in this testimony. I also gave them a presentation of the *My City, God's City* process. There was a high degree of interest in pressing ahead with the idea of implementing prayer evangelism in Bemidji.

There have now been several other meetings in Bemidji. I brought Chuck Ripka of Elk River to one of those meetings and he spoke as a marketplace leader to Bemidji marketplace leaders. Another time I brought Pastor Jay Bunker of Elk River who spoke as a pastor to Bemidji pastors. As a result of these meetings, a leadership team was formed by the pastors in Bemidji. This leadership team is composed of the following: Pastor Steve Thompson of Mt. Zion Church (in the City of Bemidji), Pastor Vern Lathe of First Assembly of God Church (in the City of Bemidji), Pastor John Werlein of Becida Community Church (in the City of Becida). This team is currently ready to set a date in order to implement the seven steps of cohesiveness described in the *My City, God's City* booklet.

Spooner and Shell Lake, Wisconsin

Michael Miller, Administrative Coordinator for Washburn County (headquartered in the City of Shell Lake, Wisconsin) participated in the *Anointed For Business* Seminar held at Crystal Evangelical Free Church (in the City of New Hope, Minnesota) during December of 2002.

Michael and I talked by phone shortly after that seminar. During that phone call he told me how he and several of his friends were implementing *Anointed For Business* study groups in their area. I told Michael that I would enjoy visiting his area and meeting with some of the pastors to see if they were interested in pursuing the process of implementing prayer evangelism in their area.

Michael and his wife Angelique invited their pastor, Pastor Virgil Amundson of Shell Lake Full Gospel Church (in the City of Shell Lake, WI), Pastor Bob Otto of Cornerstone Church (in the City of Spooner, WI), and Tom and Chris Clements, a marketplace couple within Spooner. We met for dinner in a restaurant in Spooner.

When the waitress took our orders, I told her that we were going to pray before eating and that we wanted to pray for her during that prayer. I asked her if she had a need that we could take to the Lord in prayer. She gave us her prayer request and I asked her if she would mind joining us while we prayed. She agreed, so we all held hands while we prayed. The Lord manifested His presence in that circle and the waitress was visibly moved.

Later, there was a significant anointing upon the testimony about how the leaders in Elk River had implemented prayer evangelism. I remember thinking, *The Lord is validating my testimony.* I made another visit to Spooner and Shell Lake. At that time, Pastor John Malone, of Northwoods Community Church, (in the City of Solon Springs, Wisconsin), participated. Pastor Malone said that he had an immediate witness to the idea that God wanted them to implement prayer evangelism in their area.

During the weekend of January 30-31, 2004, I taught a *Thank God It's Monday!* Seminar, based on a book I have written by the same name. Pastors Amundson, Otto and Malone participated in this seminar along with key leaders from among their congregations. Pastor Craig Nelson of Calvary Lutheran Church (in the City of Minong, Wisconsin), also participated. This seminar was a direct result of sharing the Elk River story with the pastors. During this weekend, the number of believers interested in implementing prayer evangelism in this area grew dramatically.

Meetings in Elk River during February 26-29, 2004

Ed Silvoso held a series of meetings in Elk River during this time frame. The first meeting was the Apostolic Transformation Network (ATN) meeting, which brought committed practitioners of prayer evangelism and marketplace transformation from all over the world. The second meeting was an Advanced *Anointed For Business* Seminar. There was also a united worship and marketplace commissioning service following the *Anointed For Business* Seminar. In addition, a Transformation Seminar was conducted in Spanish for Spanish-speaking pastors and their congregations. This book, *The Elk River Story,* was available for the first time at these meetings. The essence of these meetings and the book about Elk River is that this testimony is being spread to a much wider audience. Elk River is truly serving as a detonator city.

CHAPTER 20
A City Interceding for Other Cities

BY RICK HEEREN

We understand that God has placed within cities and regions a purpose for existence, or what has come to be called a "redemptive gift." That gift is not for the benefit of the city. Rather the city is to use its gift for the good of other cities. We have discerned during this process that Elk River is a city with the redemptive gift of servant.

The gift of service is found in the list of seven gifts in Romans 12:6-8. Servants serve! Give them a towel and a basin of water and they will wash your feet. They are the opposite of the ruler gift—the ruler gift likes to lead things—likes to be in charge.

A servant city

Because the servant does not covet leadership, or authority, the Lord seems to entrust this gift with a significant amount of spiritual authority, particularly in the area of intercession. This gift, for instance, has the highest anointing for demolishing strongholds. Minneapolis has the gift of giving, but needs help battling the stronghold that brings premature death to new ventures and ministries. Elk River is helping. The gift of service also has the highest authority to pray for leadership, therefore they have a role in praying for the state government in St. Paul.

The Ku Klux Klan

A couple of years ago, we were shocked to hear that the Ku Klux Klan wanted to do a rally on the steps of our State Capitol in St. Paul. I called Ken Beaudry, in Elk River, and asked him if the intercessors in Elk River would be willing to do a 24-hour prayer vigil, interceding for the City of St. Paul while the KKK was there. Ken and his wife Carrie agreed to lead this effort. Other intercessory prayer meetings were convened throughout the Twin Cities. I personally participated in a multicultural prayer gathering in St. Paul.

The Church in Elk River mobilized a 24-hour prayer vigil for the City of St. Paul to respond to the KKK visit. Following the KKK presentation, Ken and Carrie Beaudry sent a mature team of Elk River intercessors to cleanse the spiritual defilement (left by the KKK), from the steps of the State Capitol.

Praying for state government

In Chapter 22, we describe how Chuck Ripka, a businessman from Elk River, mobilized seven prayer journeys into the State Capitol. As 2004 is a major election year, the Church in Elk River will be an integral part of praying for the electoral process.

Praying for Minneapolis

As stated above, Minneapolis has the gift of giving. The essence of this gift is that it should be involved in birthing new things. I once read that Minneapolis is one of the top cities in America for creating new business ventures. Elk River is poised to protect those new ventures.

CHAPTER 21
A City Interceding for Those in Authority

BY CHUCK RIPKA

The Lord awakened me one night and unfolded a plan to bring public officials of our city, county, and state together for a time of prayer and blessing from the pastors and marketplace leaders of Elk River. I called each official that the Lord had told me to invite and nearly every one agreed to come for prayer. On January 16th, 2001, a dozen of these public officials joined us in our regular Tuesday prayer meeting and allowed us to pray for their "felt needs."

We also believe that the church in Elk River is called to intercede for public officials in our State Capitol in St. Paul. We have made a strategic friendship with Pastor Lonnie Titus who is the Chaplain to the Minnesota House of Representatives. With his assistance we have already completed four trips to the State Capitol building to pray for those in authority there.

December, 2000, Praying for elected officials

The Lord woke me up and showed me a vision of many people in the Elk River Library. There were far more people in the vision than I had ever seen before. More than just the Elk River pastors who pray there each Tuesday. I asked the Lord, "Who are all these people?" The Lord told me, "Mary Kiffmeyer, Minnesota Secretary of State; Stephanie Klinzing, Elk River Mayor; Bruce Anderson, Sheriff of Sherburne County; Tom Zerwas, Elk River Chief of Police; Phil Hall, Elk River Director of Parks and Streets; Lori Johnson, Elk River Director of Finance; David Flannery, Elk River Superintendent of Schools; and Jim Voight, Principal of Elk River High School. The Lord said, "Call them up, invite them to the Library on Tuesday at 12 noon, then sit them in a circle and lay hands on them and pray for their "felt needs."

The Lord told me to tell them exactly what He had told me. I would call up the Chief of Police, and tell him that the Lord had told me to invite him to a prayer meeting where the pastors and marketplace leaders of Elk River would pray for the "felt needs" of his position in the police force. I did this for each person that the Lord told me to invite, and they all agreed to participate.

As we all met on January 16, 2001, these people were all in a circle and they all gave us their prayer requests. For instance, Tom Zerwas said that he had two prayer requests: (1) to shut down a methamphetamine lab, and (2) to apprehend four juveniles that are raising havoc around the city. We laid hands on him and prayed for these two prayer requests. Within two weeks, the police busted that Meth-lab, and within a month, the four juveniles were caught and sent to a juvenile detention center.

So I asked the Lord, "Why are you having me do these things?" He answered, "One, it is your responsibility, and two, I am going to answer their prayer requests so they will know that you know My voice and so they will know that I know your voice." The Lord said, "I am going to give you favor with the leadership of your community, because I am going to ask you to ask them to do something in the future that they would not normally do. But they will do it because of the favor that I have given you."

Similarly, the Sheriff of Sherburne County asked for a chaplain for the County and that came to pass. Superintendent of Schools, David Flannery told us that he was about to retire and he asked us to pray for his replacement. We asked him to pray and then we agreed with his prayer. Then some months later we welcomed that replacement, Dr. Alan Jensen, into Elk River. I called Alan Jensen and asked him to come to the pastors' prayer meeting so that we could see the man that the Lord had brought into Elk River.

Eight months later we had these same people come back and give testimony about the answers to these prayers.

CHAPTER 22
A City Interceding for the State

BY CHUCK RIPKA

The Lord told me one day, "Chuck, I want more than just Elk River. I want the State of Minnesota." I responded, "The State of Minnesota, how do I go about that?" He said, "I want you to go to the State Capitol and do the same thing that you have been doing in Elk River."

Well, I didn't know anyone at the State Capitol. But I asked my friend, Rick Heeren, from Harvest Evangelism, if he knew anyone there. He told me to call Lonnie Titus who is the Chaplain to the Minnesota House of Representatives. So I called Lonnie on the phone and we arranged to have lunch together. In June, 2000 I asked Lonnie if we could start prayer walking the State Capitol building. He said, "That's strange, no one has ever asked before. Let me go ask."

He came back to me and said that permission had been granted for us to prayer walk the House of Representatives within the State Capitol on July 10, 2000. I began to invite people to join me in this prayer effort. The Lord told me that we were also to drive a wooden stake with Scripture written on it into the grounds of the State Capitol. An intercessor came to me and told me that she felt that we were to involve Minnesota Secretary of State Mary Kiffmeyer to participate in this prayer effort. I contacted Mary and she agreed to join us in the

July 10th prayer meeting. Many others, pastors and marketplace Christians alike, all agreed to come to this prayer meeting in the Capitol.

Before we went into the capitol building, Dan Adler led Rick Heeren, Pastor Paul Salfrank, myself, and about 25 other pastors in worship. As we worshiped, the Lord gave me a vision. In this vision I saw Jesus standing in the State of Minnesota. I could see the borders clearly. I saw Jesus pick up St. Paul in His left hand and Minneapolis in His right hand. He raised up St. Paul toward heaven and asked the Father, "Will you give me St. Paul?" And the Father said, "Yes!" And then raised Minneapolis toward heaven and He asked the Father, "Will you give me Minneapolis?" And the Father said, "Yes!" And then I asked the Lord, "Why was St. Paul the first city that you asked for?" And Jesus answered, "Because St. Paul was the first born." He said, "I give honor to the first born of these Twin Cities." Then the Lord reached down and picked up another city and He raised that city toward heaven and said, "Father, if you gave me St. Paul and Minneapolis, will you give Me this third city?" And the Father responded, "Yes, I will give you this third city." Then Jesus proceeded throughout the State of Minnesota picking up and asking the Father for each city, and for each town. And the Father said, "Yes," to each city and to each town. And the Lord said, "Now, Chuck, you will be in a 'state of revival.' "

Then when we finally got to the Capitol on July 10th, I felt a strong demonic presence within that building. I asked the Lord, "Would you please release two of your warring angels to go into the capitol before us?" And I saw these two twenty foot high angels. One had a sword and one had a huge hammer, or mallet. And as they walked in they caught a demon that looked like a Pan god from Greek mythology. It was half man and half animal. And they bound its hands behind its back and then laid it down on a block of granite and then crushed its skull with the hammer. And as its head was being crushed, the Lord showed me the hand of the demon. And as its head was being crushed, its hands opened up and a gold key fell from its hand to the ground. And the Lord said to me, "Now, with this key, no door will be locked to you."

We had over 100 people in the chambers of the House of Representatives. I asked Rick Heeren and Ken Beaudry to lead the ministry that night. And the Lord began to reveal to me what He wanted done that evening. He told me, "My heart grieves because there has been a separation between church and state. But My heart grieves even more because there has been a separation between church and church."

Amazingly, without my telling them anything, Rick Heeren and Secretary of State Mary Kiffmeyer did identificational repentance, repenting to each other for the separation between church and state. Rick also brought representatives forward from the various denominations and then led them to do identificational repentance to each other, repenting and asking forgiveness for the separation between church and church.

Then Rick led us in identificational repentance for sins that were committed against the various races. The first repentance was to the Jewish people. Rick asked Rabbi Ed Rothman and his wife, Alberta, of the Seed of Abraham Messianic congregation to come to the front of the room. Then Rick read a declaration that had been written by Cindy Jacobs, of the US Strategic Prayer Network, confessing and repenting for sins that had been committed against the Jewish people. Rabbi

Rothman extended forgiveness and then Rick gave him a copy of the declaration.

Then it was time to repent to representatives of the Native American people group. A couple people came forward who had some Native American blood and then Rick knelt in front of them and confessed and repented for the sins that have been committed against the First Nations people.

The last act of identificational repentance was between the generations. Rick called all of the young people to the front of the room and then a group of older people repented to the younger people for sins that had been committed by older people against younger people. All of this happened in a spirit of worship as Dan Adler from Heart of the City was there with his guitar and led us in worship throughout the evening.

Lonnie Titus subsequently told me that the staff of the Capitol told him that the atmosphere was changed as a result of what was done during that first prayer walk. Later the Lord told me, "Chuck, I want you to go into the capitol seven times. I want you to demolish the strongholds over the State of Minnesota."

On a later visit, the Lord spoke to me and said, "Chuck, do you remember the key that I gave you? It's time to go into the chambers of the Senate and the Supreme Court." So I contacted Lonnie Titus and told him that it was time to go into the Senate and Supreme Court. Lonnie responded, "It isn't possible to get into those places." I was on my way down to the capitol at that time, so I called Lonnie on my cell phone and asked him if he had gotten permission to go into the Senate and the Supreme Court. Lonnie told me that he hadn't even asked because permission is never given to enter those places. I told Lonnie that I had been given a specific word from the

Lord that no door would be locked to me and that the Lord had told me to gain access to the Senate and Supreme Court. I encouraged him to pursue authorization.

When I arrived at the capitol, Lonnie told me that when he had gone to ask permission to enter the Senate, the man who was on duty that evening was a man that Lonnie had prayed for about one year earlier. The Lord gave Lonnie favor and that man said that he would open the Senate for Lonnie. Then I told Lonnie that this was an awesome outcome, but that we still needed to get into the Supreme Court. After some discussion, Lonnie pursued this authorization and obtained it. During that visit, on March 16, 2001 we were able to pray through the House, the Senate and the Supreme Court.

The seventh visit to the State Capitol was on Friday night, September 7, 20001. Ed Silvoso and Mary Kiffmeyer, Secretary of State, were there that night. We began by releasing a group of homing pigeons from the steps of the State Capitol. We had 109 people accompany us on that trip, standing in the Rotunda, with flags and instruments, walking through the Supreme Court, into the House of Representatives, and through the tunnel to the State Office Building. As we entered, the Lord told me, "Those angels that went into the Capitol with you that first time, they are still there."

CHAPTER 23
WHERE DO WE GO FROM HERE?

BY RICK HEEREN

In Luke 19:10, Jesus makes a statement about His purpose for coming to this earth that has been long underestimated: "for the Son of Man has come to seek and to save that which was lost."

Up to now, we (the Church) have largely sold ourselves short on the full impact of that statement. The key is in the word, "that." The question to pose is, "What was 'that which was lost'?" The answer has three parts. Man was lost (sin separated him from the presence of God), man's fraternal relationships were lost (Cain killed Abel), and the relationship with his "marketplace" was lost (he was cast out of the garden and the gates were locked). In other words, that Jesus' atonement was not only meant to redeem a person, but also to restore his relationships and transform his environment.

The story of Elk River is validating what we have come to see from Luke 19:10. People are being restored to the family of God. Human relationships are being healed at every level, from the personal to the corporate, in Body of Christ and in the community. And the marketplace is being affected for the better. Government is operating more efficiently and more compassionately. The environment for education is vastly improved. Increasing numbers of business people are operating in the power and fullness of the Holy Spirit and are seeing themselves and the way they do business as catalysts for transformation in their community.

The answer to the question, "Where are we going from here?" is, "We are going for 'that which' Jesus has redeemed." All three aspects of Christ's redemptive work must continue to be pursued. At the personal level, we still have people in Elk River who are not on their way to heaven. That is why we have adopted prayer evangelism as a lifestyle—a constant that we keep practicing until the end of our days or the end of the age.

You have noticed in the preceding chapters that while evangelistic events have been referred to, rather than being the focal point of our energies and resources they have been wonderful bright spots on a continuum of constants. The constants are a) keeping the unity of the Spirit in the bond of peace, and b) filling up the city with the knowledge of God by means of a massive movement of prayer rising from the most basic relational levels.

We have found over and over again that when we pray with people for their felt needs, God shows up and does something deeper that grips the heart and makes it so natural to ask the question, "What is keeping you from receiving Jesus as your Savior right now? Wouldn't you like to?" With this happening increasingly all over our city, the effect is wearing down the enemy and loosing our community from his grip.

At the relational level, there are both challenges and opportunities. Speaking into family and marriage issues is one of our deep felt needs. Take a look at 1 Peter 3:7:

> Husbands, likewise, dwell with *them* with understand-

ing, giving honor to the wife, as to the weaker vessel, and as *being* heirs together of the grace of life, that your prayers may not be hindered.

As I review this verse, I see that building intimacy in our marriages will release prayer in a dimension of power that we have not experienced yet. Therefore, to have potent prayer capabilities, the church will have to implement a massive strategy to repair Christian marriages.

Restoring and building relationships touches us at the city level as well. We are a servant city. As such, we have been bestowed unusual grace to bless and encourage others. Like the maid at the hotel, Elk River and her people are unassuming and unseen, but never unoccupied. When you are not around, they are doing things that will make your life easier and make you look and feel better. Elk River is that kind of city for the sake of the kingdom.

Elk River is a detonator city—a relatively small explosion that will set off a larger explosion. This book is part of that detonation. The "Can-any-good-thing-come-out-of-Elk River?" mindset is being met with a resounding, "Yes!" We must walk fully into that role, not in a prideful way, but boldly realizing that what God is doing in our city is not for our city. It is for the health, well-being and restoration of cities, states and even nations, here and around the world.

Acts 1:8 says, "But you shall receive power when the Holy Spirit has come upon you; and you shall be witnesses to Me in Jerusalem, and in all Judea and Samaria, and to the end of the earth." We know we have some measurable authority for regions and nations because we have seen the spiritual climate change in our own 'Jerusalem.' In the end, the final objective is about reaching nations. As this chapter is being written, four pastors from Pray Elk River are in Butare, Rwanda because of a common conviction that the Lord was calling them to adopt a city in Africa. "We do not know what this relationship will yield. All we know is that we can only take with us what we have in us."

When it comes to the marketplace, it is easy to see the key role that marketplace Christians have played in the development of Pray Elk River. We must go even deeper and wider. What will happen when the faith and obedience of a relative few is multiplied a hundred times—perhaps through a proliferation of hundreds of small 'marketplace transformation groups' beaming throughout the workplaces of the region as points of light Monday through Friday?

Our objective is to fill our marketplace with small and large groups of Christians who see their job as a ministry vehicle to which they have been called by God so that the gospel will reach everyone within their sphere of influence; who by coming together to pray, in and for the marketplace, will bring the presence and the power of God to it; and by doing so, will turn the lunch hour into the most extraordinary hour of spiritual power in Elk River, every day of the week.

We realize that we are at the beginning of this effort to reach Elk River for Christ. As Ken Beaudry likes to say, "We can see the corn growing, but it is only knee high." But we are driven by a fresh understanding of Romans 8:19:

> For the earnest expectation of the creation eagerly waits for the revealing of the sons of God.

Let the revelation begin!

CHAPTER 24

EPILOGUE

HOPE FOR YOU – HOPE FOR YOUR CITY

BY DAVE THOMPSON
SENIOR VICE PRESIDENT, HARVEST EVANGELISM

You have just read the story of a modern-day "70 others" much like the ones Jesus sent out in Luke Chapter 10. No big names. No heavy artillery. No credit cards. Not even a bag to carry an extra change of clothes in. They were not of the same denomination. They were not even all of the same profession. Before it all began, they hardly knew each other. They were a lot like you and me in our cities. But God found someone who was hoping, and seeking and listening. And He spoke. And He was heard. And He was obeyed. In fact, the simple story line has likely filled you with hope that maybe if this can happen in a city like Elk River, it could happen in your city, too.

In 1988, a group of pastors from Resistencia, Argentina called on our team to assist them in "reaching their city for Christ." We believed a project like this should be done, and to find out if it could be done, we needed a city in which to try it. This was the invitation we had been waiting for! We accepted, very much like a wedding ceremony. Both parties said, "I do," and off we headed into the future.

And very much like many newlyweds, none of us knew very much about what we had just gotten ourselves into. As team leader, I remember sitting in a circle with the pastors, looking at each other and asking, "Does anyone around here know how to do what we have just committed ourselves to do?" There was a moment of silence as stark reality hit full force. No, no one among us had ever done it before. And to make matters worse, there were no stories like this one to listen to, and no books to read on the subject. We were all alone.

We decided to take a bold step. We'd tell God that we didn't know how to do what He was calling us to do. I have envisioned heaven perking up at that moment, the Father, the Son and the Holy Spirit, peering down upon our perplexed and humbled group, nudging each other and whispering excitedly, "Hey, did you hear what I just heard? These guys want to reach a city but did we hear right? Did they really admit they don't know how to do it? *Maybe there is a chance for us! We know! Now, if they will only listen.*"

It may be that when you began Chapter 1, you thought, "Aha! Here's the program. If I just follow the steps and the procues, I will get a reached city, right?" Wrong. It's not a program. It's a process. It's not about activities. It's a lifestyle. If you want your city to change, you will need to change, all the way to the core of your being.

K.C. Foster tucked away a profound principle between parentheses back in Chapter 2. "By the way," he said, "let me share a word of insight here. Every application from this book needs to follow the prompting and leading of the Holy Spirit. It may look a little different from city to city, but the same basic principles will need to be in place."

If you boil everything about city reaching down to its basic principles, you've found them in the lines of this book. Hope. Seek. Listen. Obey. Do you know that for the first 18 months of our experience in Resistencia we cried out to the Lord for His strategy for the city. And for 18 months, heaven was silent on strategy. It was *not* silent, however, on the sins of divisiveness and indifference. For 18 months, God was saying, "I can't put anointing or authority into leaky buckets. If you can't love each other, I can't trust you. If you don't love each other personally and corporately, you will never learn to embrace your city, for you cannot change what you do not love."

That is why in this story there is a constant undercurrent of togetherness—seeking together, hearing together, obeying together, even suffering together. You have read about repentance being the price tag for unity, brokenness producing boldness and selfless servanthood erupting into decisive leadership. In the end the players and their city are triumphing together.

When God finally started talking to us about strategy, the strategy was prayer. In fact, one of the pastors bluntly stated, "You see how prayer has changed us? If it can do that for us, it can do it for our city. We need to fill the city with prayer." Families began to pray for their neighbors; employees began praying for their coworkers; CEO's began praying for the competitors. We needed a name for it and struck on "Lighthouses of Prayer." The name was a by-product. The love came from the heart.

When we finished our three-year commitment to "Plan Resistencia," we discovered that the city was not the same. It had changed for the better. Not only had the Church of the city grown (by 102%), but it was spoken well of among the people. It would not be until several years later that we would discover the "spiritual climate change" terminology. In fact, we were not even privy to the Luke 10 model for prayer evangelism in those days, but somehow, the Lord had led us to do it, even though in ignorance.

Knowing something dramatic had taken place, we reviewed the experience to discover what it was. That's what the book, *That None Should Perish,* was all about—the principles for reaching a city as discovered by ignorant, tenacious servants of God. In that book, Ed Silvoso identifies 6 steps to reach a city—six phases through which our committed group of city reachers went on to impact Resistencia. To this day, we have found that every thriving city reaching effort has experienced these steps.

1. Establish God's perimeter in the city

If you have something from God stirring in your heart for your city, be assured there is at least one other to whom God has been speaking—likely more. Go find them. Look to both pulpit ministers, like Paul Salfrank, Greg Pagh, Tom Ness, Percy Kallevig and Bob Pullar. And look to marketplace ministers like K.C. Foster, Ken Beaudry and Chuck Ripka. Don't look for many. Look for the ones like you.

2. Secure God's perimeter in the city

Come together. Pray together, minister to each other, to the Lord and to your city. We suggest that you do it every week. Pray. Don't plan. If you come together, Jesus will be in your midst. And if Jesus is present, He will always have something to say. Listen. Begin to work through the steps to cohesiveness that Rick Heeren mentioned in the first chapter. Let the Lord build the house so that you do not labor in vain.

3. Expand Gods' perimeter in the city

Your "warm fire" will attract others of kindred spirit. It may attract some others who want to alter, organize, politicize and usurp. Keep your focus on the presence of the Lord. Your objective is going to be to fill the city with prayer under the authority of unity. Do not lose your focus.

Don't force expansion. Let it happen, like an organism. As you work through the cohesive steps, you will be engaging leaders and workers who are themselves change agents in the marketplace. Your numbers and spheres of influence are growing exponentially and naturally.

4. Infiltrate the enemy's perimeter in the city

Mobilize massive prayer in the city for the city—families praying for their neighbors; workers for their coworkers; students for their classmates; professionals for their industry peers. We have called it "prayer evangelism"—talking to God about your neighbors before you talk to your neighbors about God. It's lobbing bombs of blessing into enemy territory. The peace of God, that passes all understanding, released by multitudes of peace speakers across the city confuses his efforts and numbers his days.

5. Attack and destroy satan's perimeter

This is where we have found the 7-day prayer evangelism exercise is so effective. Having weakened the enemy's stranglehold on the city with "air strikes," this "ground assault" is a display of corporate boldness in the city and has a similar dual effect on the city as what occurred with the disciples in the book of Acts. The Church was encouraged and emboldened, and the devil began to lose his assets to the kingdom of light. From this point on, if you do not stop, the city begins to be "filled…with your teaching."

6. Establish God's new perimeter where satan's used to be

It is very important that I clarify here what you have achieved and what you have not achieved. Wrong expectations can kill the right vision. So, do not think that you have reached your city. Barring a Jonah-like miracle, you have not. What you have done is expanded the small beachhead that you established back in Step 1. You have more Christians involved, more leaders, more workers, more congregations, more pulpit ministers and marketplace ministers, and some very brand new believers. Declare and establish it.

And then what?

Pay attention, for this is key. Step 6 is just like step one. You have a perimeter that needs to be expanded. Therefore, keep going. Take another lap. This lap will be different because you are different, the Church is different and your city is different. Beware that because you have taken on a new strategic approach to your city, satan will change his approach toward you. "New levels—new devils" is a very real maxim. Use it to your advantage. Keep close to God, to each other and to your city, and God will give it to you.

Some of you may be saying, "How do I begin?" I am drawn to the story of Gideon, which has so many insights to city reaching. This one comes from the beginning of his story. Gideon's land was being mercilessly raped and pummeled by an enemy who comes not to conquer, but only to consume—to satisfy his appetites at the expense of another. We accuse Gideon of being fearful, but I note that while Israel was hiding in the caves, Gideon was not. He was threshing wheat in a wine vat. Have you ever wondered where he got his wheat?

The Bible does not say, but it does say that God calls Gideon "a valiant warrior" and declares, "The Lord is with you." That most likely eliminates theft as an option.

I choose to believe that Gideon made a fundamental decision—something that Paul Salfrank and his wife imitated when they "married the land." One way or another, Gideon married his land, saying "no" to the enemy that was pillaging the crops of his people. If I may look in between the lines, I see Gideon declaring in spirit, *This is my land because God gave it to me. It is not the enemy's, who is illegally lodged here. I will plant in my land, I will grow a crop, I will weed and water, and I will harvest. Then I will eat bread of the fruit of my land.* What he was doing fearfully for a moment was the tangible evidence of a fearless commitment so powerful as to grab heaven's attention.

And God came down, and watched.

These men and women of Elk River are daring to give their reputations and even their lives for their city. They are catching heaven's attention, and God keeps coming down to meet them. And do you know what they know? They know that what God is doing in Elk River is not for Elk River. It's for you. Beyond that, what God is doing in Elk River is not just for you either. It's for the healing of entire nations. That's why it must happen in your city. There is a nation or two out there depending on it.

I challenge you. Dare to hope. Dare to seek. Dare to listen. Dare to obey.

Pray with me this prayer:

Lord Jesus, Your Word says that you came to seek and to save that which was lost. What Adam lost in his sin and I in mine was not only my relationship to you, which you have restored, but also my relationship to my fellow man and beyond that to my "garden"—the place of provision and sustenance that my city is. I declare to you now that I want to see my city restored and transformed by the same powerful redemption that You provided for me. I want to be part of that transformation. I am willing to pay whatever the price may be, but my city shall be called the city of the Most High God. Would You transform me so that You can use me to transform my city? From this moment on, my life is in Your hands, for the sake of my city. In Your matchless name, Amen!

CONTACT INFORMATION

Harvest Evangelism, Inc.
Midwest Region
Nehemiah Center
810 S. 7th Street
Minneapolis, MN 55415

612-278-1737
HarvestMidwest@aol.com

Harvest Evangelism, Inc.
International Headquarters
P.O. Box 20310
San Jose, CA 95160-0310

408-927-9052
www.harvestevan.org